BREAK HER

A DARK BEAUTY AND THE BEAST FANTASY ROMANCE

TRANSFORMATION TRILOGY
BOOK TWO

CASSIE ALEXANDER

This is a work of fiction. Names, characters, places, and incidents are a product of the author's imagination. Locales and public names are sometimes used for atmospheric purposes. Any resemblance to actual people, living or dead, or to businesses, companies, events, institutions, or locales is completely coincidental.

www.cassiealexander.com

Cover by the Bookbrander.

Interior hardcover art by IV Benjamin.

Formatting by Morrigan Author Services.

“Those who restrain desire do so because theirs is weak enough to be restrained.”

—William Blake

PROLOGUE
LISANE

I ran to the hallway to stop him, but I was too late—Rhaim had portaled away, leaving me alone in his castle, while he went off to kill my father.

I turned to the wall and pounded a fist upon it, and then groaned. I was still sore from working magic earlier. I put a hand beneath my breast to where my ribs ached—the tub's waters hadn't healed me completely, but I was out of magic now.

And I was trapped here, unable to stop his vengeance. I wasn't strong enough on my own, because my magic didn't work unless someone else had hurt me.

Rhaim's name for me was right—compared to him, I was a moth.

Something beautiful, but easily crushed.

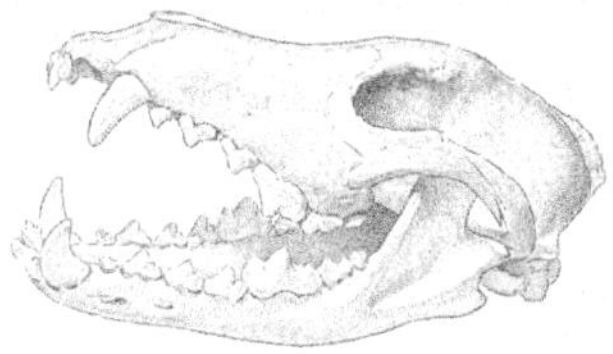

1

RHAIM

I didn't portal directly to Jaegar's war tent—instead, I moved from place to place miles away in the surrounding countryside, in the dark, using my magic to pull the wolves that I knew were there closer to the outskirts of the camp and human firelight.

And when I was finished, I portaled myself to a spot in front of Jaegar's tent. His nightly guards saw me, but none of them appeared concerned—they knew who I was, and by now they were used to the odd comings and goings of other mages—and Jaegar likely hadn't told them they were going to war with one. I summoned one of the owls that nested nearby to eat the rodents that such a large encampment encouraged, and it came to me, still carrying the gold ring I'd bent around its foot the day before. I pried this object off of it and set it free, waiting patiently for my plan to come together, even as I seethed with the need to act.

Jaegar had thought he'd take Lisane away from me? After having given her to me in the first place?

And all because she had *chosen* my company over his?

I hadn't read the letter from her I'd delivered to him, thinking myself above it at the time, but now I wished I had—I would've read the sentence where she said she wasn't returning a thousand times.

As it was—I reached out with my mind and heard several distant howls. My creatures were in their places.

"I call a convocation!" I shouted aloud.

Jaegar's guards, who'd begun to eye me with curiosity, startled. They had no idea what a convocation meant—but other mages would, and I knew Jaegar's throne-sworn slept nearby.

Castillion the Spiked came out of the next tent over, shirtless and half-awake. "A convocation? On what grounds?"

"Your king tried to steal from me." I watched him with glittering eyes, waiting for him to try to deny it. The obvious question would've been to ask "Steal what?" but we both knew Castillion didn't need to guess. He'd been the one to deliver a sleeping Lisane to me two months prior.

There were more howls now, as wolves spoke to other wolves, and I heard the clamor and surprise of men waking to the sound.

"All-Beast," Castillion complained, after waving his hand toward Jaegar's tent, sending one of Jaegar's guards scurrying inside.

"Do you deny it?" I took a broad step forward. My beast hated him to an irrational degree, and I felt its pull inside me, asking to be set loose.

Castillion's jaw ground and I knew the man hated me back. "I have no idea what you're talking about," he spat.

My eyes narrowed. I knew Castillion was Jaegar's closest mage—and it didn't sound like he was lying. My rational, mannish part wanted to gather more information to understand, whereas my beast thought Castillion would quickly confess if he were made to see his own intestines.

Other mages gathered, whomever was at camp and not out on missions fighting the Deathless—the war against the monsters was a round-the-clock operation, seeing that as of yet no one could predict when they'd attack. I heard them murmuring concerns to one another, giving me wide berth, and I saw Sibyi the Cloudmaker join their ranks, leaning heavily on his staff, still healing after having recently broken his leg.

I waited until my wolves' howls reached a crescendo, making it clear that the entire camp was surrounded by creatures loyal only to me, and then with a gesture from my hand, their howling stopped, leaving ominous silence behind.

"You all know I had no interest in the lives of men," I said, addressing my fellow mages solely, though I knew soldiers beyond them would hear as well. If this camp had just been full of soldiers, I would have killed them all in thoughtless retribution for trying to steal Lisane, but I knew I needed to prove my case to those who were of my kind. "And perhaps some of you know that for years, Jaegar tried to tempt me into his battles, offering what I suspect he offered most of you. Gold, power, opportunities for greatness—things I needed none of, or that I already possessed."

I saw Castillion's eyes widen as he realized what I would share next.

"A day before I joined your ranks, Jaegar made a bargain with me. He had Castillion deposit his daughter, Lisane, outside my castle, for me to do with as I please, and I have fought for him ever since."

There were gasps at this. Castillion stepped forward, the spikes he was named for rippling across his naked chest, metal piercing through his skin, and my beast longed to answer his challenge. "Rhaim!" he shouted.

"I let her think you dead, rather than a disappointment!" I snarled as the howls outside of camp started up again, louder, closer, as I summoned the wolves to me.

Castillion shot a spike out through one palm, where he could use it like a sword.

"Rhaim called convocation!" Sibyi shouted. "He's not done talking!"

"Indeed," I agreed. And if Castillion attacked me now, I would have the right to kill him—and in the unlikely event he survived the attack, other mages would shun him for the rest of his days. So I slowly turned and made sure my voice would carry. "I have been side by side with many of you. I have saved some of your lives, to be sure, and at least a thousand Deathless have been murdered by my hands," I said, and raised an arm into the air, clawing my fingers into a fist.

"And yet," I said, finishing my circuit, to face Jaegar who had finally emerged from his tent, "*And yet*—yesterday he betrayed me. Sent men to attack me at my castle. To try to take what is *mine* back."

"I did no such thing," Jaegar proclaimed.

I laughed harshly as the wolves I'd called in raced through the camp, scaring the circle of lesser mages who kept the camp safe from the Deathless. I could see through the wolves eyes as the men they encountered jumped back in terror. "Have you no honor?" I asked Jaegar.

Helkin, Jaegar's son and Lisane's brother, ran up—and he had somehow known to put all of his armor on. "He has more honor than you do, monster!"

No. I wasn't monstrous, yet—but I soon would be. "You *gave* her to *me,*" I growled, my deep voice going rough as I started to change, my bones bending and pushing out into my far more frightening form, half again as big as any human could be, covered in muscle and short dark fur. "She is *mine.*" I laid claim to her, even as my mouth crowded with teeth. "And anyone who tries to take her from me *will be punished.*"

I snaked my head around to include everyone else who was near. I wanted them all to know. Now that Lisane was within my castle, and within my grasp—

"I am never releasing her," I snarled, and then focused my attention back on Jaegar. "Ask him the truth of things. He knows she is happy."

Jaegar's spine was made of steel—and I knew he was where Lisane had gotten her stubbornness from. But I still had his ring in my palm, as proof of having delivered Lisane's letter. All the men here would recognize the markings on it, even though it was bent, if he made me show it to them.

He stared me down. "Happy—no," he said, and then took a deep inhale. "But she does want to stay with you, All-Beast, for now."

And it was my turn to seem unbothered, even though I was. My beast didn't care if Lisane was happy, so long as she was *his*—but the man in me took the news of her unhappiness like a blow, even as I understood its cause.

I had hurt her.

Many times now, on purpose. That she was willing to *be* hurt didn't change that fact.

The first of my wolves reached the center of camp, leaping in to sit by my side, calmly panting with his tongue lolling out, as more wove through tents to join him. Nosy soldiers on the perimeter shouted and shirked back, while Jaegar and Helkin's guards crowded closer. I didn't want the wolves to get injured, so I hadn't told them that they should be angry —yet—as they circled me.

"Father, how can you say that?" Helkin gasped, whirling to look at the man.

"She wrote me a letter that Rhaim was so kind as to deliver recently."

Helkin appeared horrified by this, and I began to guess the truth of things. Lisane hadn't lied to me when she'd told me she'd wanted to stay...and Jaegar wasn't likely lying about his ignorance, now that he was confessing the letter's existence, and as much as admitting to our bargain, before the whole camp.

Which left Helkin and his friend Vethys, Lisane's former betrothed, whose corpse was now feeding fish in the Azurlean Sea. I took a step toward the boy, as the wolves nearest me took to snarling. Castillion leapt in front of him, his spike-sword out.

"Where is your friend?" I asked Helkin, jerking my jaw up. "The one your age, with the purple cross on his breastplate?"

"I don't know," he lied—but I could scent his fear with my own nose and the noses of the surrounding wolves.

"Well, if you don't know, then I certainly don't know, either," I said, and gave him a menacing smile. Let Vethys's people come to Jaegar and wonder what happened to their floating battleship and child. Let him explain to them that I killed every single man aboard, including their son—because his own son had sent him to me. "But let me ask you this—do you truly want her back, or do you just not want me to have her?"

Helkin didn't answer.

If my beast were left alone with him...the wolves nearest me began growling, matching *his* mood.

But I needed to become a man again eventually and face Lisane. If she were already unhappy now, discovering that I had killed members of her family would not endear me further, no matter how richly they deserved it.

I turned away from him and spoke to my fellow mages first. "Do not trust the soldiers or your king," I said, before sneering up at Jaegar. "Our bargain is broken." And then I addressed anyone who could hear me. "Anyone else who dares trespass against me, to try to take what is *mine*," I said, snarling as the wolves did, "will never know peace again, not even as a corpse, because once you are dead I will have jackals shake your body apart and vultures strip your bones."

The wolves began a raucous howling, punctuating my curse from both inside and outside of camp, and I joined them, my beast's voice every bit as wild as theirs. I had thought I'd portal elsewhere after this, to bide my time until I was in full control of myself again, but decided against it. I didn't want to leave the wolves in danger here among the soldiers—I put Jaegar's ring in my mouth, and raced out of camp with them on all fours.

I wanted everyone present to see me for who I truly was—no man, but the All-Beast.

2

LISANE

For three days, any time I walked through the library I was reminded of the destruction that I'd caused. The massive, jagged anchor that Vethys's ship had shot into Rhaim's floating castle to link the two structures was still there, like the castle had been attacked by some giant iron buck, who had rammed it with its horns. A portion of the library had been destroyed, and much of what was left was in utter chaos, books scattered after having fallen from their shelves when the castle tilted while under attack.

I made a start at fixing things, putting books into piles by size, and sweeping up broken glass. Even Finx tried to help—mostly by using his webbing to pin down stacks of papers so they didn't get blown out the shattered wall—but it felt endless, and pointless, too.

I didn't know when—*or even if!*—Rhaim was coming back, or how I would feel when he returned.

"Did he say anything?" I asked Finx, who I thought might know Rhaim's comings and goings better than me. Maybe he'd been in the hallway before I'd made it out, and had scurried off before I could spot him.

"No," Finx said, bobbing his entire body apologetically, a black bristly ball suspended between all eight of his legs. "He never really does."

And Rhaim's continued absence gave me too much time to think.

Every night I sat at my vanity, opened up my journal, dipped my feathered pen into the inkwell, and hesitated while my empty pages taunted me.

Was I, or was I not, going to continue with this madness?

There was no guessing anymore—Vethys hurting me had led directly to my being able to do magic against him. I definitively knew what my magic's cost was.

And, knowing that, it was possible I could just go out into the world and wait for violence to be flung upon me, and practice it that way, slowly and horribly, catch-as-catch can...

Or I could stay here and train with Rhaim.

With intention.

Which would mean letting *him* hurt me.

A task which he'd seemed all too eager to do, even before I knew the confines of my magic.

I pressed a hand beneath my breast, to where my ribs had broken. My body didn't ache anymore—I'd soaked outdoors in the healing tub often enough to get better, and made sure to rest and eat, like Rhaim always told me to—but my mind was another matter.

If I wasn't going to continue training, then I could stop writing in my journal right now.

If I was...then I had to come to grips with my current situation: being beholden to Rhaim.

In a way, nothing had changed, because I already had been, had I not? It wasn't like there were any other mages interested in teaching me.

But knowing that I needed him to make myself magical chafed. It felt like my powers were requiring me to build my own prison—a feeling I did spend the time to draw in my journal, rather than trust it with words, sketching a small birdcage with a moth hovering inside it.

He'd once told me that great magic had great costs, and I knew from my studies that every true mage paid them. My cost seemed inherently high to me, especially because I did not want to be reined. But if I guessed right, Rhaim's beast was the cost of his. I remembered the creature he'd been in his library, dark and heated, with wild eyes, and I knew it was that version of him that my father...was facing? Had faced?

Was Helkin burying him right now?

I didn't know, and I didn't like that.

But there was no denying that Rhaim's magic was great.

So might mine be, too?

...or was I just to be punished because this was what happened when women were taught?

I didn't know, and if Rhaim was telling the truth that he didn't either, I suspected no one did. I looked at my hand and frowned, wondering if fire might catch up with me.

It wasn't that I was even afraid of getting hurt. It was that it would have to be *him*, again, and again. It seemed utterly unfair that he should have so much control over me—and more so after whatever it was that he'd done to me in the tub. My hand still went at night to cup the place between my legs where he'd licked me, my fingers touching the same places that he had with his tongue. I hadn't managed to make myself feel like he had yet, and I wondered if the sensations he'd pulled from me then were another kind of cruel magery.

How could the man that made me feel so good be the same man I needed to be cruel to me?

It wasn't the kind of question I wanted to write in my journal.

On the fourth day, after I came out upstairs from my room and ate a little from the pantry, I found him in the library, leveraging the anchor out with his own brute strength.

I stood in the doorway, watching him, and he knew I was there. "You could help, you know," he said, even though he'd almost managed it.

There was a harsh scraping as the last prong clawed through the hardwood riser, and then the horrible thing was free. The castle tilted, spilling some of the piles of books I'd carefully balanced, before righting itself again. Rhaim dusted off his hands before turning back to me. He was wearing his familiar black leathers, and he seemed entirely intact.

My father's men hadn't even gotten in a blow.

"Get dressed," he told me.

"I am dressed," I said. I was wearing some of the delicate dresses Finx had made me like I always did here.

He shook his head subtly. "Not enough to go outside. I'll go get you things," he said, then opened a portal, and disappeared.

Outside? I wondered—and then ran up to the hole the anchor had left to look out and down. The castle was descending at an alarming rate, following the same path the anchor had, to the middle of a grassy field.

I had been on the roof of the castle many times now, but I hadn't been outside to walk on the ground in...I didn't even know how long. And at the thought of being outdoors, with the earth beneath my feet—I ran for the stairwell and my bedroom.

There were boots that fit me placed beside my bed, and a heavy cloak that did not placed atop it. I pulled it on, and realized it had been meant for Rhaim—it trailed behind me every step I took, like the train of a coronation gown. I ran downstairs, which was where I imagined the exit from Rhaim's castle was, and I'd guessed right; he was already there.

"Would you like to walk, or would you like to ride?" he asked.

"Ride," I answered without hesitation. He nodded, and pushed open a heavy wooden door, revealing an antechamber and another door—one more layer of protection from prying eyes—and then past it, the outer world.

"We will have to walk some first, but our horses will catch up," he said, locking both doors behind him and then boldly taking off into the surrounding field. I hurried after him. We'd landed in the center of some kind of grain crop. I looked back at the castle, all the better to finally get to see it from the outside, and realized there were several floors of it I'd never been to. And then I realized that his cloak's train was leaving a wide trail of destruction behind me, breaking fragile stems of fresh growth.

"Will we pay someone for this damage?" I asked him.

"Better yet," he said. "I'll give them the gift of compliant bees." I nodded, and then I stopped. I couldn't pretend that nothing had happened since I'd seen him last. He stopped too, several steps ahead of me. "Your father still lives," he said, without looking back.

I swallowed. "And my brother?"

"Regrettably," he said, and started walking again.

I knew I might never see either of them again in person, but it still mattered to me. I didn't think Rhaim would lie...and the next time I had magic, I could find a mirror to spy on them through. Until then, I would take Rhaim at his word.

I picked up his cloak like I might a dress's skirt, and followed after him.

An hour later, I was sore, and we were on a road and the bottom of Rhaim's cloak was ruined with dust, but I didn't care.

I was outside!

Periodically, I would stop and look up at the sun, just because I could, my eyes closed, turning toward it like I had read that flowers would. Other times I would reach out on the side of the road, brushing my fingers through whatever was growing there, the peeling white bark of young saplings, touching the dark green foliage on their branches that trailed down. I heard the sounds of water from far away, and wanted to angle toward it, but Rhaim said we would be near it soon enough.

He always walked ahead of me, leading, but he stayed close and didn't rush me, even though I knew he must have had a goal.

I was considering asking him about it, when a pair of horses trotted up. One was a massive piebald workhorse, with a neck so big I couldn't have gotten my arms around it, and the other was a very docile-looking mare with a milk-white coat. She kept her head swung low, but her eyes were curious and bright.

I had only been on a horse once before, as a child—my father had lifted me up onto his saddle to show me off to our people for his amusement, and until now it had been one of the best memories of my life.

"But...where are the..." I gestured towards their empty backs.

"Riding with me, you do not need one," Rhaim said. He picked me up without warning and placed me on the white horse sidesaddle, pushing my front leg crooked so it was very nearly astride her. I had a moment of panic until I'd bound my hands into her mane. She was content to stand there, as Rhaim vaulted onto his piebald horse's back.

"A gentled mare, eh?" I asked him, risking letting go for long enough to pet her.

He looked over at me then, his gaze fully catching mine for the first time since his return.

"Gentler than some," he said, and both our horses started walking. "Loosen your hips to move as she does, and you'll be less sore tomorrow."

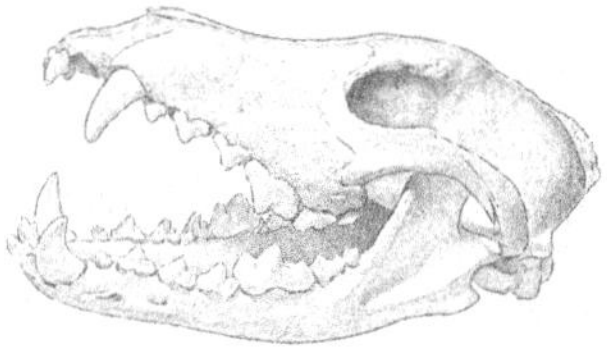

3
RHAIM

Watching Lisane in the world was heartbreaking.

I didn't need to watch her with my own eyes, not when the countryside was verdant, from voles in the fields to birds in the air. Instead, I watched her through the eyes of a hundred different creatures, each with their own way of seeing, and used these images, feelings, and sensations to paint a picture of her in my mind.

The way she wanted to interact with everything she encountered, and how she found plebeian objects entertaining, touching stones and leaves and bark—it was charming, but also deeply sad.

I had known in an abstract way that the fate of high-born women was grim, but watching Lisane pause to watch a caterpillar like a child made me wish I could go back in time —not just to three days ago to murder Jaegar, but back to when Lisane was younger, to tear his castle apart and pull her out of it.

"The water!" she said, as the road veered near. Our horse's hooves clattered over a wooden bridge above a stream and then I heard her gasp, spotting the small town on the horizon.

It was a place I had been welcomed before, and I knew they had craftsmen capable of doing my castle's repairs. I bid my horse to stop while hers caught up, and spied a series of little braids in her horse's mane, like she did in her own hair. "Have you been to a town before?" I couldn't believe I was asking, and yet...

She frowned—for the first time that day. *I had kept her happy, for a few hours, at least.* "To a town, yes. In a town...not really," she said.

I nodded at her. "Stay near me, then. Follow my lead. And don't run off."

"Where would I go?" she asked, half irritated and half curious.

"I don't know," I said. "You might follow a butterfly." I meant it as a tease, but from her crestfallen look, she did not take it well, so I rephrased. "You will be with me, little moth, and so few men will dare to so much as look your way. But you are as lovely as I am cruel, so it would not be kind to tempt them. Hold on." I gestured toward her horse's mane again, and she took hold of it with a squeal as the mare fell into a rolling trot beneath her. Mine trotted at a much more stately pace at her side. "I would like to eat someone else's cooking tonight," I told her. "Wouldn't you?"

The shadow of fear flew from her face as she found her seat on the mare and then flashed me a grin—pleased more with her own competence than with me. "Yes," she agreed.

"And buy fresh cheeses and fine cloth?"

"Cheese, yes," she said, before giving me a bemused look. "But no matter what you do, you can't make me sew."

"What if I told you mages had to sew?" I asked as my horse jogged beside hers.

"I've read too many of their journals to believe that, so I would call you a liar," she said, in a haughty tone, with a smirk—her version of teasing me.

It was good enough.

"Would you like to go faster?"

Her eyes lit up. "Always."

I brought both horses to a stop, and pulled mine directly alongside hers. "Let go," I warned her, grabbing her waist and pulling her over her horse and behind me, sidesaddle, onto mine. She managed to not kick her mare as I settled her. "Now, hold on," I said, turning forward again.

She hesitated—I could see as much through the mare's eyes, as she teetered, trying to find her balance without touching me. Luckily the horse's back was wide. Finally she announced, "I'm still mad at you."

I smiled and managed not to chuckle, though it was a close thing. "Truly?" I asked, in the most sarcastic tone.

"You—" she started, her words drifting. "You can't imagine what it felt like when the anchor came through the wall."

The seriousness of her voice wiped the smile from my face. I nudged the horse beneath us forward into a slow walk with my mind. "Then tell me."

She was silent for a long time. "It felt like I was going to die."

I curled my hands into fists but kept them low, where she couldn't see. Would Helkin truly have rather seen her dead than ceded her to me? Just as I was on the verge of pressing her for more, she began a story.

"Every time I went outside as a child was for an event. This was after my brother had aged out of being protected in chambers and got his own room above, and I hadn't fully accepted yet that I never would. On those rare occasions, my mother would put me in new dresses, supervise maids who did my hair, and tell me how to act."

"And did you listen to her?" I asked, watching her head bow with memories, through the mare's eyes.

"Sometimes. Other times, I acted like a child—because I was one, and I was so mad that my brother got to leave, but not me." She paused again, sifting through her memories. "Each time those things happened though, whatever it was that required our family being paraded around, my mother would start to be tired or say her feet hurt, near the end of it. Then, when we came back to our rooms, she would stay up for hours, or seem perfectly sound."

I remained quiet, wondering where my little moth's story was going.

"It took me years to realize that she wasn't tired or aching, or even modeling good behavior for me. No, I think, although I didn't get the chance to ask her before she died—but *I think* —she couldn't stand the thought of being told when she was to be put back away. Like a doll picked up, then returned to the shelf, hardly played with. She wanted to be in control of her own fate, and that was the only way she could manage it."

I wished I'd left Lisane upon the other horse, so she could more easily see the stricken face I was making on behalf of her child self—but maybe it was easier for her to confess, safely hidden behind me.

"At the thought of going back to be put onto a shelf," she continued quietly. "I couldn't have borne it. When Vethys pried me from the castle, I thought hope was lost. I would have rather tumbled to the sea than be put away again."

"Lisane," I murmured.

"And I am still not recovered from that," she said, speaking over me.

I let the moment resonate between us as it deserved to, even as it humbled me. What would have happened if I had been a minute slower? I knew I was supposed to see her terrified face before I died—my Ascension had warned me as much—but nothing about it implied she had to be alive at the time, and I knew I was fully capable of torturing myself with memories.

"Nor should you be," I agreed softly, much later.

She made an affirmative sound. "And then?" she continued. "Your beast appeared to save me. Which I was glad of, until I saw him again."

I had known a reckoning for *him* was coming. *His* time with her in the library had been fraught with bloodlust and unchecked desires—and the terror in her amber eyes wouldn't have held *him* back, except that unlike my little moth, my beast had no wish to die. "My beast is the price of my magic," I admitted. "That is not an excuse for him, however."

I watched her frown again through the mare. "Nor is it an apology."

"One should only apologize for things you can guarantee not to repeat." I felt her tense at that, as she accidentally kneed our mount, and I weighed my pride against her safety. I didn't want to have to admit to *him* also being *me*, but I did need to tell her something because there was a chance she killed me while I was being beastly and deserved it. "You should know his intentions toward you are not good."

"I had noticed," she said, her voice small, which pained me, but I continued regardless.

"And if you see him again, you should probably run."

I could see her now through the mare's eyes, holding herself and staring daggers at the back of my head so strongly it was a wonder I did not feel them. I sighed. "I would never set him loose on you on purpose, Lisane. But just as you cannot control how your magic is powered, neither can I mine. I am sorry to have scared you, though."

She snorted to let me know just what she thought of that, and my horse walked in silence for a long while, as quiet as its riders. I had no idea what she was thinking, the mare had fallen back. Had memories of my beast poisoned whatever well of tolerance I'd filled within her? Or had something happened in the days since I left her naked in her bed, to make her change her mind about me?

Other than her thinking me capable of regicide?

I looked over my shoulder and spoke curtly. "You may still be mad at me if we go quickly. Then we'd at least have the advantage of getting there before nightfall."

She huffed again at that. But eventually, she unlaced her arms and wrapped them around me, pressing herself against my back, and while she may have regretted the necessity, she didn't flinch when one of my hands found hers and pressed it tight to hold her there.

"Don't let go," I told her. I felt her nod her cheek against my back, and we took off.

4

LISANE

It wasn't comfortable riding sidesaddle and clinging to Rhaim, blinking strands of his hair from my eyes.

But for all that I hated him—and I was fairly sure I still did—he'd brought me here.

Outside.

I wished I could see more of the countryside—between Rhaim's broad back and how fast we were going, it was hard—but the sensation of speed was exhilarating, and the knowledge that we were going into a town thrilled me.

And then when we were in it and the horse slowed, my head nearly swiveled off my neck.

Chickens scratched at the ground between the legs of goats, a fat dog ran by being chased by a skinny cat, and I was grinning wildly. It smelled, yes, and everything was a little dirty...but there were people walking by, men and women, freely mingling, children playing, someone's mother scolding them for not coming in...

This was the life I had only read about in books.

Rhaim's horses walked in parallel down a scuffed road, stopping when we reached a two-story stone-and-wood building near its center—and he was still holding my hand, his fingers almost twined with mine. I let go of him, pushing back. "Hop down," he suggested, twisting to give me his arm. I took it, feeling his rock-like muscles as I briefly held onto it, dropping to the ground.

My feet squished into the thinnest layer of mud—and I remembered to whip the bottom of the cloak up out of it a second too late.

Rhaim made the horse sidestep away from me, and then dismounted himself. The horses seemed perfectly happy to just stand outside of the building we were in front of. Rhaim walked in, and I followed behind closely.

Even more people were indoors, gathered around low tables, eating dinner, and one of them squealed at seeing Rhaim. "Kind sir!" she said, running up to him and barely stopping out of touching range. She was an older woman, around the same age my mother had been when she had died.

Rhaim squinted at her. "Pella?"

"You remember! After all these years!" She took his arm, ignoring me, and announced him to the room. "The beast mage is here!"

Rhaim shirked back at that. "I am here to resupply, and to get repairs."

She gave him a lively glance. "And you'll have them, if only you'll trade!"

He heaved a belabored sigh, but gave her an indulgent look. "If it comes with your two finest rooms, you've got a deal."

"I'll go kick the men in them out right now!"

I hovered behind him, watching news of his arrival spread through the room, and one of the men nearest cleared his throat first, stepping away from his table and up to Rhaim. "I've heard of you, sir. I've got a—"

"I would eat first, and make arrangements." Rhaim held up his hand to stop him. "But the construction on my castle will likely take several days. I will make time to talk to all before leaving." The man shoved his hands into his pockets, but then he nodded, and Rhaim looked across the room, until he spotted a little boy. "Are you from here?" he asked.

"Yes!" the child said, catching onto the general excitement.

“Please tell me whose horses I have borrowed—the two standing outside—I would like to repay them,” he said, and flipped a coin in the child’s direction. He caught it, fumbled it, and then caught it again, before running out with a smile.

There was the sound of a commotion, coming down the open stair. “Pella, I can’t believe you—into the cold, dark night?”

“The stable’s plenty warm!” Pella was telling the man she was shooing down, who was half-dressed, with several bags about his shoulders. Then she shouted, “Girl!” and a woman not any older than I was popped her head out of the back kitchen. “Go change the sheets!”

“They get fresh sheets, too?” the half-dressed man complained, shrugging on his shirt then buttoning his jacket, before he spotted Rhaim and squinted. “Bully,” he chided, then stared. “Wait—you’re the one they talk about. Big lad, all dressed in leathers, talks to animals? I thought my mother made that story up!” He clapped his empty hand on his thigh. “I’ve got a lame horse—”

“Tomorrow,” Rhaim said, cutting him off, taking my arm to pull me to the stairs.

“Well, I’ll be in the stable, so you’ll know where to find me,” the man called after us, casting a glance at me, and I heard him mutter "Aye, if I was with her, I'd want a room too" as we passed.

I followed Rhaim into his room, not knowing where else to go. The other girl was there, hurrying to freshen his sheets. She had raven black hair and the tanned skin of a woman who'd been allowed to walk around freely her whole life, and when she was done with the sheets she gave Rhaim an appraising glance. "I don't charge very much, sir," she said, looking at him with half-lidded eyes, and I didn't like the way *sir* sounded, coming off her tongue.

"And yet, it would still be not enough—but also too rich, for the likes of me," Rhaim said, giving her a courteous nod.

She briefly pouted. "You'll tell me when you change your mind, sir? There's another girl here—she's no good."

"*If* I change my mind, you will be the one I seek."

Her pout lifted into a smile. "Very well then, sir," she said, and looked to me. "Come along then, girl. Your room's across the hall."

"She may wait until after we eat," Rhaim said.

“Of course, sir,” the woman said. “Pella will bring up food momentarily, if they’re not slaughtering a lamb in your honor.”

“Please don’t. Any food will do,” Rhaim said, and gestured her out the door, closing it behind her.

I took a moment to look around the room, before confronting him. The bed would barely fit me, and the table near it had been carved into by guests before. There was no chair, there were no books—“This isn’t much of a bedroom, is it?”

“Not really, no,” Rhaim agreed. “I think that’s the same table I saw here thirty years ago, and possibly the same sheets,” he said, sitting on the bed itself. “But they’re trying.”

I glanced out the door the women had left through. “Why am I in a different room?” I asked, looking back at him.

He shrugged. “Sometimes it’s hard for me to judge how angry you are, little moth. I thought it safer to assume you didn’t want to be in my room with me.”

Even if I had...there was hardly room for him in this one room, much less space for two.

“And what was she offering you?” I asked. I thought I knew, but I wanted to hear it from his lips. I felt compelled to know.

“What do you think?” he asked in return, narrowing his eyes, as his mouth curved into a sly smile.

"Herself," I answered.

Rhaim nodded. "Indeed."

I frowned at him. "Have you done that before?"

He put his arms behind himself on the bed and rocked back, watching me coolly. "I don't make a practice of it, but yes. It seems only fair to compensate people after suffering my attentions."

"Suffering being the operative word." We also hadn't discussed the matter of my magic or my training, since his return—or any of the other things he'd done. "You shouldn't have read my journal."

"That was wrong of me, I agree. I won't do it again; I swear it."

I crossed my arms. "That's not good enough. I want to read yours."

Rhaim's eyes widened, and he snorted. "Sir," he said, "I want to read yours *sir*, and no, you cannot."

"Why not?"

"*Sir*," he added, for me. "Because I have been alive for far too long, and because today you've apparently lost your manners."

I lifted my chin, all the better to stare down my nose at him. "Why does it matter if I call you sir or not, seeing as anyone can?"

"Ahh." He chuckled as I felt myself lightly flush. "Because her sirs cost her nothing, little moth—whereas I know precisely what they cost you."

His gaze was steady on mine. The last time I had called him *sir*, he'd had his mouth between my legs, and we both knew I'd wanted him to keep it there. I swallowed.

"Then when do we resume my training...sir?" I made myself sound as aloof as I possibly could.

Rhaim seemed to consider it for a moment and then shook his head dismissively. "Not now, moth. I need to deal with the damage to my castle first, and we might as well resupply while we're at it." Then he looked at me, with one eyebrow cocked up. "And if you were to cry out tonight, that other woman might get upset," he said, a barbed tease.

I stared him down. "Nothing you could do to me could make me scream."

His nostrils flared and for a second I thought I was in danger of his beast coming out and joining me, then he turned his head to the door. "We will have to test that—later," he told me, and then more loudly said, "Come in," right as someone knocked and Pella brought in a wide tray holding plates.

CHAPTER 4

I was more hungry than I thought I'd be, sitting on his bed with him, as far away as I could be while still able to reach the food.

"Do you have any other questions, moth?" he asked, ripping into a piece of rough dark bread.

"How long will we be here?"

"At least a week. I'll pay the men extra to work around the clock, but acquiring the beams alone will take several days."

"And what will I do?"

"What would you like to do?" he asked, watching me out of the corner of his eye as he drank the beer the woman had brought.

"To ride again."

"Of course. No horse will ever do you harm when I am near. What else?"

What else? The truth was, I didn't know, I was so out of my element. Telling Rhaim I wanted to walk around freely outdoors and sit in front of a fire with strangers, to do things that others had clearly been allowed to do their whole life, felt silly.

Worse yet—it made me feel small.

"There is plenty of time to decide if you're feeling overwhelmed," he said, pushing himself back on his bed and beginning to kick off his boots. "If you're done eating, perhaps you'd like to visit your own room now?"

I nodded and stood, dusting crumbs off my fingers against his cloak, then paused. I felt full of things I wanted to say.

Did you mean what you said in the tub about not always hurting me?

Will you still hurt me when I need you to—but then make me feel like that again?

Not without me begging, most likely, I thought darkly.

"Moth?" he inquired.

"Nothing," I said with a head shake, and left the room.

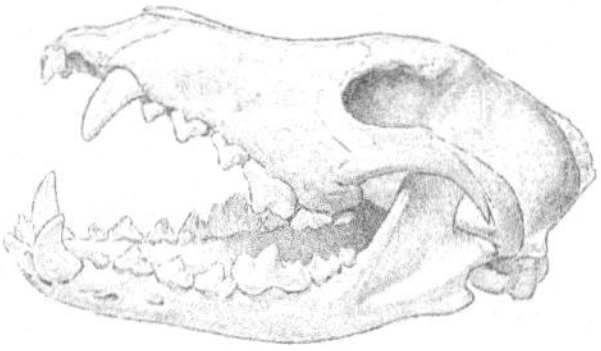

5
RHAIM

I put the empty tray back in the hall, closed the door, and then took off my shirt, making myself as comfortable in the small bed as I could and before quenching the lamp light.

The whole room smelled like Lisane—and horse, but I could concentrate on the former. Watching my moth deal with even the smallest amount of jealousy had been delightful.

Not because I wanted to discomfort her, but because it allowed me to pretend for a moment that somehow, if I played my cards exceedingly carefully, that I might be able to keep her.

I would never be able to tell her of the bargain I'd made with her father, of course. But unlike him, I wouldn't make Lisane stay with me if she didn't want to.

And I would give her reason upon reason to stay, if she would but let me…and if me giving her those reasons didn't chase her off.

I lay in the dark, listening to the snores of strangers through the thin walls and feeling the restlessness of the creatures in the stable outside. The moon was high, so foxes were prowling, cats too, and somewhere in a nearby field, a hardy ewe was giving birth.

This was one of the reasons I mostly put my castle down in desolate places. So that I could concentrate on my own studies, rather than be sundered into pieces, listening and feeling every bit of information that my magic funneled in. If I concentrated too hard, I'd hear the termites in the walls, or whatever tiny hair-clinging pests that girl who'd offered herself undoubtedly carried.

It made it difficult to relax, even when I was tired…but I knew what would soothe me. I thought about denying myself, but only for a moment, then my hands were on the leather laces of my pants, quickly unstringing them until I was free.

I took myself in hand and rolled my soft sheath over my already hard cock—all I had to do was think about bringing any part of myself near the place on Lisane I'd licked, and I began to throb.

I wanted to kiss her sweet lips, to taste her tongue, to feel the beat of her pulse beneath my teeth at her neck and breast—but more than anything else I wanted to be inside her.

I stroked myself up and down, imagining what would've happened if I hadn't denied her in the tub, if I'd been just a little less strong. Her hair had been wildly strewn over towels and stone, her face flushed with want, her hips curved with need, and I had made her pussy as juicy and plump as a summer peach, ripe for me to take.

She had even *asked* for me to cover her.

Not fully knowing what it meant—and never having done it before.

Just feeling the ache inside her where she wanted me to be.

And at the thought of doing so—I made a tighter fist around my head, shifting the ring there to the side, imagining what it would feel like to push into her molten heat for the first time. Feeling her stretch, listening to her breath catch as I pierced her, the small gasp she'd make when she was uncomfortable, and then the welcoming sigh she would make when that was through.

And then the long, slow slide inside her, as I pushed my way in, reading her face and body like a book, applying just enough force and tension to keep her deliciously aware of this new space in her body that belonged to me alone, as I claimed it.

I slid my grip down to my hilt, and used the other to cup my heavy balls.

Could she handle me? I had to believe that she could—because every time I was around her, I felt the need to make her mine. And I didn't just want her perfect cunt—I wanted every inch of her. Her mouth, her ass—she'd lost my collar, but I wanted to rope her with my cum. I wanted to fuck her so thoroughly that any man who saw her in the future—after she had, somehow, caused my death—would know that she'd been mine.

I wanted her to feel extraordinary things by my hands: the pricking of my claws, the mark of my palm, the bite of my fangs. I wanted to bind her with rope and torture her with my tongue until she begged to come or be set free, cut her down, rub her with silk till she stopped mewling, and then tie her up again.

I wanted to mark her inside and out.

I wanted to take her apart and put her back together again.

And when I was finished with her—I was using both my hands on myself now, rolling up and down my shaft, breathing hard, trying to hold it in and back—*and when I was finished with her*—when I had made her cry out not only *sir* but *my name* and felt her clench and shake around me until she couldn't remember her own—I would bury my cock deep inside her like I was meant to and fill her to the teeth with my cum and seal her cunt around me with my *knot.*

I gasped as hot jets of seed spattered against my chest and stomach, my cock twitching as my balls pumped and more blood surged, sending the base of me swelling to the size of two clasped hands, and it was my turn to feel stretched as I groaned. I let go of myself, panting, my hot, taut cock curved atop my stomach, and I trailed fingertips up and down the slight, sensitive ridge on its belly, while my balls gave a final spasm, pushing one last burst of cum out of my slit to briefly pool on my stomach before slowly trailing down my side.

Fresh sheets indeed.

I laughed darkly at myself. I had no way to clean myself up—but I didn't care. I could close my eyes now—I didn't feel the other nearby creatures anymore, just the contented thudding of my own heart, beating, *mine-mine-mine.*

6

LISANE

Rhaim was right. I was sore when I got up—my leg muscles ached and my hips were tight.

But we were still someplace new and close to being outside. I got up and crossed the hall to look for him, knocking at his door. He didn't answer, so I decided to creep downstairs.

"You're up!" the older woman from the prior night said, spotting me on the stairway. "I'll get your breakfast. Please, sit down."

I went to where she gestured. The room was empty now, the fire cold, and when she returned, she caught my curious observations.

"Everyone's outside now, talking to the Beast Man," she said with a grin, putting a plate of eggs down in front of me, along with biscuits and a mug of something hot.

I grinned back at her; I couldn't help myself. "You mean the All-Beast," I corrected her.

"Oh, is that how he fancies himself?" she said and laughed. "I'll make a note. What's your name, and why do you travel with him?"

I opened my mouth to tell her, then wondered if I shouldn't. I had some small knowledge of geography, but I had no idea what this town's name was, or if it was within my country's borders. "Lirane," I said, giving her the name of the very pure girl my mother had made me read about as a child rather than my own. "And I travel with him because he's training me."

A furrow appeared between Pella's eyes. "In what?"

I inhaled. I couldn't tell her magic, because she'd think I was a liar. But I didn't have anything else that I was good at.

She reached out to pat my arm. "It's okay, girl. If *training* is what they're calling it nowadays in the fancy places, far be it from me to stop you two, if you both enjoy what you're doing."

I thought back to all the many times Rhaim had hurt me. "Enjoy isn't perhaps the right word," I admitted, feeling sheepish.

"But you're here of your own accord?" she asked, appearing suddenly concerned for me. I nodded quickly and she grunted, then reached out to fondle a lock of my hair. "Well, a pretty girl like you could fetch a lot. Too much for the likes of here. And I bet it's better to be with him than with others, eh?"

The truth was, I had no idea, but agreement seemed necessary to end this conversation. "Yes," I said as though I believed it, and she let me finish eating quietly.

When I was finished, I went outside, expecting to have to look for Rhaim, but he hadn't gone far—he'd set himself up at the edge of a well in the town center—but there were wall-to-wall creatures, people and animals both, between us. Right now there was a goat in his lap, and he was talking to a man who I presumed was its owner. We were separated by several sheep, four horses, more chickens than I could count, and I heard bells around cows' necks as they queued past a bend.

Then he looked up and spotted me, and animals in front of me opened up to make a path. I flipped the hood of his cloak up and started walking to his side—I wanted to see him work his magic, close up.

The animals' owners, however, had not gotten the message. "Eh, wait your turn," the first man I encountered said, not realizing his beasts had stepped several feet over.

"I've been here since dawn!" grumbled another, blocking my path with his shepherd's crook.

How rude! I took the end of it, tempted to use it to push him back, then I heard Rhaim's voice.

"Hold," he said, and the final animals between us parted, like an opening book.

"I'm expected, excuse me," I said, glaring at the man who'd blocked me, walking up to Rhaim's side. He set the goat down and stood, clapping his hands to dust them as I arrived.

"I want them to see you," he said quietly, reaching up to push the cloak's hood back. And then more loudly, he began, "This is—"

"Lirane," I whispered quickly.

He smiled down at me, remembering. "Does that mean you're going to faint?" he teased in a low voice.

"Not hardly," I quietly promised. The morning light softened his strong features, as did the amused look he was giving me, and his smile rippled the tail end of the scar I had given him. It was light now, his skin tougher than I had hoped, but I would always know where it was, in my heart, and what it stood for—the first time I had hurt him with my magic.

I could feel everyone's attention behind me, like a weighted breath, and Rhaim looked over my shoulder. "This is Lirane, my consort," he announced. "Please treat her as you would me."

I stiffened, glad there was no one to see my surprise but the recently dropped goat. "I am no such thing," I hissed at him.

The corners of his smile took a sharper turn. "Later, moth, later," he advised and gestured for the next farmer to step up.

I stood beside him for a time, feeling humiliated, and wondering if that was his goal—then wondering if I could channel it into power. I tried, imagining a ghostly hand strangling his throat, but other than him once giving me a curious look, it seemed to have no effect.

As for him...farmers came to him with questions, showed him lame horses, and brought in breeding stock. A woman walked away in tears when she found out her favorite milking cow was going to die soon—there was nothing for it—while a man gloated that he would get his prize bull branded with a mage-mark hand, to denote that it'd been blessed.

During all these occurrences, Rhaim was kind but stern, doling out advice, harsh truths, and magical aid in equal measure, taking the time to hold or touch whatever beast they brought near, with the same gentleness and care he'd taken with me that one night. I didn't know whether or not to be jealous that his touches seemed the same.

"That's enough, that's enough," Pella said at midday, bringing out a pan to hit with a metal spoon. "Let the mage eat and rest!"

People grumbled and discussed the best way to keep their places in line while also breaking as little girls swept geese Rhaim had worked on away. He'd promised to make them fertile until such a time as they were eaten, when they would be deliciously full of fat and juice, as long as they'd been well cared for up 'til then.

"Is that really magic?" I wondered as the crowd thinned a bit. "Of course they'll lay more, if they're treated right."

"Not always...but you're not wrong. Sometimes the magic is in the idea I plant in their heads—a little extra straw, or grain, or they take care to make sure their fence is sewn up against the foxes."

I pondered this for a moment. "Then who guards over wild creatures? Is it so fair that you help all of these beasts here, just because they're owned? What happens to that fox?"

"I often wonder about that myself," he said, standing with a stretch. "I do what I can, as I pass." He made to walk toward the inn, but I stopped him.

"I'm not your consort, Rhaim." I didn't know what I was—but I wasn't that. It was bad enough the innkeeper had assumed this morning, and now the whole town would.

He nodded. "Are we friends, though?" he asked, tinging his words with curiosity.

I couldn't name us that, either. I frowned. "You could've called me your apprentice."

Both his eyebrows arched. "These people have remembered me for thirty years. Do you not think they'd remember a story of a woman studying to be a mage? Plus, there's only so many intrusions from the outside world I can protect us from, and we both know that me teaching you is not allowed."

"I haven't caught on fire yet," I muttered. A dark look crossed his face, and whatever horror I'd felt at him naming me his consort was tripled now, as I considered the fact that he might not be willing to train me at all. "So...you will train me tonight?" I asked, trying to keep my panic from my voice.

"No," he said, and held up a hand before I could fight him. "You alone know what this kindness is costing me, little moth." Rhaim glanced around at the animals people had left in the square. "I would not visit my beast on these people, or on you."

I swallowed down the knot in my throat and reached for the only weapon I currently had—my tongue. "And here I was thinking you were talking about how hard it was for you to appear personable for several consecutive minutes."

He snorted softly. "That too," he said, then gestured me ahead of himself, toward the inn, but I shook my head.

"No. If I go inside, people will think that I'm with you."

"Would that be so bad?" His expression was entirely neutral.

"Going from being owned to being bought?" I asked in a rising hiss. "Yes!"

Rhaim scoffed. "As if any man could afford you," he said, then shrugged. "Do not go too far."

He turned and I watched him walk into the building. I heard people cheering as he entered the inn, but I had a feeling he would be eating by himself in his room.

And then I realized that for the first time in my entire life, I was alone outside.

To say I didn't know what to do next was an understatement. I had a strange sense of freedom that was also a little frightening as I looked around at the people doing their business in the square.

I already knew it wouldn't do to act like I had on the road here—the people who'd been around last night and this morning were far too sensible and busy to stop and look at excitingly colored beetles, and I knew better than to be unruly in public from my royal upbringing.

But there were still things to see and do, and people to talk to.

And for their part...they were ready to talk to me.

"Girl—let me give you a flower!" said an old woman, walking up, with boughs of flowers in a basket at her hip.

She pulled out an ivory-colored bloom, all curved petals and elegance, and handed it to me.

I took it from her, then she appeared to be waiting, and I remembered Rhaim giving the boy coin the prior night. "I don't have any money," I said, before trying to give the flower back, feeling slightly humiliated by my first solo experience in the outside world already.

"Nonsense, it's yours," she said, briefly cupping my hand around the stem, as she gave me a toothless smile.

I smiled back at her then stepped away and there was already another person waiting there, a man with a type of fruit I'd never seen before, quickly paring it for me. "I—I couldn't, possibly," I said, backing up further, and then strode off in a direction like I knew where I was going and what I was doing.

But it was too late.

Between Rhaim's comment at the well, and how haplessly I'd just acted, the entire town knew they could *buy* him—*I guessed?*—through me.

A man came up to offer me a wooden toy, for a child I didn't have, and I took it accidentally, unable to give it back before he disappeared. Then my hands were full, which meant that a woman brought a basket out to me, and after that people just kept putting things into it. A laced shawl, jars of preserves, a beautiful glass bottle that I assumed held liquor or perfume—I didn't get a chance to ask the owner which, as I slowly became overburdened. I hadn't even gotten into any stores on my own, and now I was afraid to. What if the store owner just gave me the keys?

"Thank you very much. I appreciate it," I said repeatedly, trying to be gracious, now heading back to the tavern we were staying at, but it was like heading upstream—and then when I got closer, I saw the animals had retaken their places, which meant Rhaim's break was through—and if he saw me like this, he would be too amused for me to stand.

"I'm going to rest now, thank you," I said, flagging back the people who were still following me...just to see where I would go? What I would do? Was this what being a mage was like? I aimed for the tavern, then took a sharp right, to travel down its side. Maybe if I left town, I would be free.

A door on the tavern's wall opened up, and the dark-haired girl from the night before caught me. She was wearing the exact same thing she'd had on prior, only now there was a basket of linens under one of her arms, and she gave me and all the things I held a *look*.

"I feel very silly," I confessed, all of her sir-ish sins forgotten, so long as she would treat me plain.

She took in my overburdened state and warmly laughed. "Do you need some help?"

"Yes. Please."

She looked over my shoulder for a second, and whistled. "Eh! Give the girl a break!" she commanded my last stragglers, and then to me, she said, "Come on."

I walked alongside her without question. "I'm Jelena," she announced, tossing back a lock of black hair. She had tiny silver hoops in her ears, the kind my mother would've been outraged by if she saw them on a maid.

I loved them instantly.

"I'm Lirane," I said, remembering in time to keep my lie up.

She grinned. "I know. I heard."

"So did everyone else," I said with dismay.

"It's not often we get ladies here. They're just a little bit in awe."

I heaved the basket into one hand and put the other on my forehead. Was that what I was now? It angered me that I couldn't claim to be a mage—and that every title I could give myself was only by association with some man. Then I looked to her. "Why aren't you?"

She made a wry face. "I empty the buckets from your room, scrape the food from your bowls, and wash the sheets that you sleep on," she said, shrugging the basket she carried. "It's hard to think people are special when you see them up close-like. Plus, you spoke to me first," she said, with a solid nod.

"I did," I agreed quickly. "I like your earrings."

Jelena beamed at me. "I know where you can get some."

I followed Jelena readily, listening to her talk as we reached the river and walked along its bank. She mostly wanted to know where I had traveled; she'd lived in this town her whole life.

"I've seen a lot of places." At least I could say that, now, truthfully. "But I haven't been out in many of them. Past the town where I grew up, I mean," I lied, praying she wouldn't ask me for more details. "It's on the other side of the continent." I waved a hand towards the horizon. "But I've seen snow! And mountains. And we've floated over the middle of the sea."

"So it's true his castle flies?"

"It does."

She blew air through pursed lips, considering this. "Are oceans as big as they say?"

"It seems like it, from the sky."

Jelena gave a thoughtful nod. "If you walk down the river far enough, there's a place where it's so wide you can't see across it anymore. I wonder if it's like that?"

"I suspect it is."

"Well," she said, punctuating our conversation, and casting a long glance behind us. "I think it's safe for you to go back now."

I felt her words like a mortal blow. I knew we weren't friends—I wasn't that naïve—but I also did not want to return to the dollhouse yet. I drew up straighter and braced myself. "I would rather not."

The look she gave me was mystified. "I'm going to do laundry in the river," she explained, like that should be enough.

And for any other girl it would be. But I had never been *in* a river, nor *done* laundry, and I had a sudden strong desire to do both. I needed to learn how to work in the world, and my magic was not the type that made the world kinder for me. "I can help," I offered.

Jelena looked at me as though I'd grown a second head. "If you really want to, I won't stop you," she said slowly.

"That's good," I told her, settling down and smiling sweetly. "Because mostly? No one can."

Jelena took me at my word and directed us to the riverbank, where there were already two women our age working, swinging sticks that looked like oars. A sturdy blonde girl with a round face noticed us first.

"Oy! About time you got here!" she said, pointing her stick at Jelena and I. She was in the shallows barefoot, with her skirt tied up, standing in front of a bench full of fabric with a wide paddle in her hand.

The other stopped mid-swing. Her hair, eyes, and skin were all similar shades of brown. "Shush, Treneth—you know how Jelena likes to sleep in," she said, with an emphasis on the word *sleep*.

"You're just jealous because I've got more than one job," Jelena said, cocking her hip with the laundry on it out—then she reached out to pull me forward. "Plus, I brought help!"

I opened my mouth in sudden fear. "That might be overselling it," I warned. "But I'm willing." And then I looked at the surrounding beach, filled with drying linens, underthings, and shirts. These girls had been here all morning, and they had probably missed Rhaim's outburst. I fished in the basket. "I have bread, jam, and possibly liquor," I said, hefting the glass bottle full of brown fluid up to show. "Teach me?"

Treneth put her paddle down, leaned on it, and gave me an appraising glance. "Anyone willing to work, I'm willing to train. But you'd better be prepared to get some blisters, princess."

I froze for a second, wondering if they knew—and cursing myself for not coming up with a different, better name—but then I realized she was using princess as a derogatory term.

That, at least, was something we could agree on.

I started taking off my boots at once.

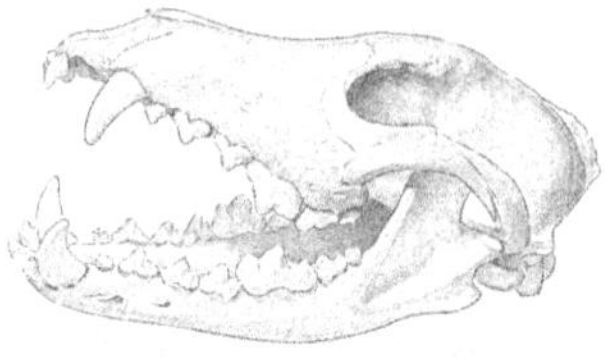

7
RHAIM

If I had to purge worms out of one more creature's ass, I was going to roar.

It was truly challenging being so polite for so long, and soon I wasn't going to be able to manage it.

But news of my arrival had spread to the surrounding countryside, and even now more shepherds were guiding their flocks in.

Thankfully, Pella rescued me halfway through the afternoon, securing herself a spot in my good graces and several large gemstones in the future. I begged away from the remaining husbandry types and took the food she offered me up to my room, where I could safely concentrate, and the first thing I did once there was check on Lisane.

I set my mind on the birds I'd sent to follow her, and they showed me images of her sitting on a riverbank...smacking things with sticks. I was perplexed by this, but she was with other girls, and they were laughing together, which made me smile. I had no idea what it was that she was doing, but it seemed fitting that hitting things suited her temperament.

After that, and when I was done eating, I portaled back to my castle, and exited the portal room to find Finx on the floor of my laboratory waiting for me, chittering angrily.

He accosted me at once. "Where have you been?!"

I locked the door to the portal chamber behind me. "Coordinating supplies. Has construction started yet?" I'd met with the foreman of a work crew before I started my magery in the morning. "And did you seal off the rest of the library like I asked you to?"

Finx huffed. "I did. But they're still out there. I can hear them talking, and they are *poking* things." I noticed he was sitting on a nexus of webbing, in the center of the floor, stroking his paws out over multiple strands in turn. "There!" he exclaimed. "They're doing it now!"

"Show me," I told him, and he leapt up to the wall and ran out of the room, all too eager to tattle on the intruders.

Strands of Finx's web led down the stairs to the library, which was on my castle's fourth floor. Finx had created a barrier of thick webbing between the undamaged inside, and the outside world, and men were moving around on the other side of it, sometimes brushing up against his wall.

"See?" Finx complained, pointing a paw out at their shadows.

"Shh," I said, putting a finger to my lips. It was better they thought the castle occupied only by spiders than haunted. "Seal this up behind me," I told him, hooking a finger into the webbing, to tear it open so I could pass through. Men on the other side gasped as I emerged, and then their eyes widened further yet, at seeing Finx's large shadow closing the webbing up from the other side. "I wanted to see how things were coming along," I announced, standing on the narrow ledge of space Finx's protective web had left them. It pained me to see my castle in such splintered disarray, but it'd required repairs before and would likely again in the future.

One of the workers whistled down, and I heard the sound of men's grunts, and rope twisting in a pulley. It pulled up a board caged by ropes, and with it, the foreman Ajeil, who looked much like his father and his grandfather before him had, short and with a chest the circumference of an oaken barrel. "Mage!" he said, stepping off of the board and onto the castle's narrow edge to join me. "We just finished scaffolding this morning—and now we're doing measurements. We don't want to bring the wrong size of wood up."

"Will you be able to source it quickly?"

"There's several more mills along the river, since you last visited."

I grunted. "Good."

"I'm glad you're here, though—I wanted to ask you if we could get more space to work." He gestured at the edge of the wood we stood on. Finx chittered unhappily on the far side of the web, and I shared his concern—my castle was safer the less people saw of it, which Ajeil also knew; I'd made it quite clear when we'd begun. "Just three or four more handsbreadths would help," he said. "It would be faster with room for more people."

And the faster it was done, the faster I could take Lisane away. "I will see what my spider can do for you this evening."

Ajeil doffed his hat at that, surveyed the project—Finx's web in particular—and shook his head. "My dad always said you were a strange sort."

I didn't take offense. "It comes with the magic. I hope he also told you I pay well, and quickly."

"He did."

"Good—then do you know a man who can make me more bookcases?"

He laughed. "With enough money, all things are possible."

"I'll get you measurements for those as well, then." I was about to make my way back through the webbing to do so, when I spotted a lone storm cloud on the horizon, tight and dark, and entirely out of place in the middle of this sunny day. "You'll have to excuse me," I said, loudly enough for Finx to hear inside, and opened up a portal to as far out on the horizon as I could see.

The swaying grass I landed in was almost knee height—it would be this winter's foraging for the creatures I was tending to in town. I looked out across it and spotted the man I suspected was there, leaning on a staff and waving a welcoming hand, standing in the shadow that his cloud made. Now that I was closer I could use views of him from several nearby creatures to triangulate from, so I portaled close enough to make him jump back when I emerged.

"You're not very subtle, Cloudmaker," I announced.

"Neither are you, All-Beast!" Sibyi said, lowering the hand he'd clutched to himself in surprise. He had his robes on, and his shoulders were wrapped with the crossed belts that held his water bags.

"How did you find me?" I asked, sounding displeased.

"Would you believe that I know what your sweat tastes like when it evaporates?" He waved a hand overhead, and the cloud there began to dissipate.

I about spit on the ground. "I would prefer not to." I stretched my mind thin, sensing for dangers in this field, and keeping a very distant eye on Lisane. *If any one of Jaegar's men or mages touched her—*

"I came alone," Sibyi said, perhaps sensing my concern. "The camp has been in uproar since you left. Many of us were dissatisfied by your treatment—I thought that you should know."

And then I did spit. "I do not seek your approval or that of any others. I only wish to be left alone."

One of his eyebrows crawled so far up his forehead, it almost became hair for his bald head. "With the girl."

A low growl escaped my throat before I could stop it. "With the girl that no one cared about, ever, until she was given to me. Why are you here, Sibyi?"

"Because I have questions and I think too hard."

I groaned, knowing nothing good could come of his curiosity, and spun my hand behind me to create a portal back to town. "I don't have time for this."

He hobbled around quickly on his staff to disrupt my portal with its tip, swirling it in opposition to my hand. "You hate authority, Rhaim. You've told me as much, on more than one occasion. So why would you, the legendary All-Beast, ever take a bribe?"

"You carried my pipe tobacco, remember?" I said with a frown, but he ignored me and went on.

"And you're far too old to be swayed by a pretty girl's face. Beauty is fleeting, and you're not a fool." He stuck his staff into the ground and gave me a prim look. "So."

"So," I repeated back to him. "Give me one good reason why I shouldn't summon forth a plague of grasshoppers to kill you?"

"Because that's not how I die, Rhaim. *I* drown. And you...your death has something to do with that girl." He read my silence for the acknowledgement it was and whooped. "It's the only reason why you would bother with her! I knew it! The only one!" He wasn't accusatory; he was just pleased with himself.

"Perhaps you drown in grasshoppers," I threatened him. "After someone's hamstrung you with their claws."

"Bah!" he said, still lighthearted about it. "We're friends, Rhaim. We must be, because I know I've irritated you several times now and you haven't murdered me yet."

"That is a low bar." I stared at him flatly. "So? What of it?"

Most mages didn't want anyone to know how they would die, lest someone manage to manufacture those circumstances for you early, despite fate being involved at all times. In that way, we were a superstitious lot.

"So...do you have her trapped away somewhere? Hidden in women's chambers perhaps?" he asked, jerking his chin back at my castle. "Tended to only by your servants, and never seen by you to keep you safe?"

"You have some imagination, Sibyi."

"Oh, come on, Rhaim. Indulge me," he said, and he grinned at me with mirth. "Or, you think to make her love you so she will save you, and you mount her every night."

My hand was wrapped around his throat in a moment, what was beastly in me coming through. "I could kill you thrice before your lightning hit me," I warned him. "Bite your tongue and never talk of her again."

His eyes were wide, almost boggling out of their sockets, but I didn't scent any fear on him. I picked him up and threw him some distance away, for his own wellbeing, sending his staff flying with him.

Sibyi took his time getting up, coughing and holding his throat where I'd left a red handprint, gawking at me. "Rhaim," he said, in the same tone as my long forgotten mother, who I'd so often disappointed. "You cannot truly care for a human. You *know* that."

I started summoning grasshoppers; I didn't care how he died. "What part of 'do not speak of her' do you not understand?" I asked, flexing my hands into fists at my side as numerous small creatures started pinging against him. I wouldn't even have to murder him myself; I could sift my hands through the ground at my feet and pull any one of hundreds of violent creatures from it. He had to know that. We'd fought against the Deathless together often enough, yet still he went on.

"You cannot get her with child, Rhaim—have you told her that?" he asked, his indignity rising as he crouched down to pick up his cane. "And she will age and die, and you—you are *you*!" he said, pointing his cane at me when he'd finished standing.

"I am *what?*" I asked him, my voice a low growl of warning.

He gestured dramatically at the grasshoppers that were overrunning his feet now, twenty deep, and crawling up his legs. "The most stubborn mage I've ever met!" He reached down to sweep a hand over his robes and flick the insects off. "Stop this, or I will drown every creature in this field, including your laborers," he threatened, reaching for one of his water bags. "And good luck pulling timber through six inches of mud."

Sibyi paused before making good on his threat, as a fresh and sure-to-be-irritating fire lit inside his eyes, and he continued. "But I can work with love, Rhaim, if love indeed it may be. Or whatever passes for it inside you here," he said, waving the bag over his own chest, but meaning mine, as grasshoppers piled up to his knees. "If you do care for her, when you set her down—which we both know you someday must—surely you wouldn't abandon her to a world that the Deathless control, now, would you?"

"I have no need to deal in suppositions—"

"And if not for her, Rhaim," he cut me off, swinging the water bag wildly, "where will you get supplies in the future? Who will be around to fix your castle's walls? The Deathless continue in your absence, and you know we are not winning."

I lifted my eyes heavenward. "And you say I am the stubborn one."

“I’m only still alive because you know I’m right,” he said, finally taking a casual sip and then refastening the bag to his belt. He began walking toward me, kicking grasshoppers right and left. “So come back, Rhaim. Our interests are aligned! We would make sure that you would only go out with fellow mages. You needn’t work with soldiers—*you could even go alone!*—just as long as you were fighting on our side.” He implored me with his eyes, his tone, and one outstretched hand.

I shook his words off of me. “You attempt to be a good person, Sibyi, because your life has not beaten it out of you yet. It is more foolish than commendable.”

“I take it that’s a no?” he asked, as I turned to begin walking to my castle. “Oh, come on, Rhaim!” he shouted at my back. “Think of the girl!”

My hackles rose, but I stopped myself from growling, *I think of nothing else.*

“Fuck off, Sibyi, and don’t bother me again.” I batted an arm up and sent a fresh wave of grasshoppers at him, this time aiming them for his head. I heard him squawk a curse word before portaling away, whereas I kept walking so I could be alone with my thoughts.

8

LISANE

Every bone in my body was sore, and underneath Rhaim's cloak—the bottom of which was now soaked—all of me was covered in sweat.

But I was *happy*.

Jelena, Treneth, and Vissa, the lanky girl who I'd now met, had been cheerfully gossiping amongst themselves for the past hour in between hitting laundry on sticks and then wringing it out on the poles that I realized were set up along-side the shore for just that reason, before laying it out to dry.

"I can't stand it anymore, Lirane," Treneth said, coming back to the water's edge with another load. "It's killing me to watch you. Please take that thing off."

They'd all made noises when I'd walked into the river with Rhaim's cloak on. But I only had Finx's dresses on beneath it, which I knew were nothing like the clothes they wore, or what we laundered.

At the same time, though, the water was only making the cloak heavier, and while my soul felt lighter, my skin felt disgusting.

"Do you promise not to say anything?" I asked, and the three of them looked to each other.

Jelena made a gesture at the other two. "We do."

"All right, then." I slogged into the shore and shrugged off Rhaim's cloak. Each of them gasped, and I winced. Finx's spider-silk dresses were stunningly iridescent in the daylight, making me feel very out of place on the gray stone beach.

Jelena recovered first, guessing at the truth of things. "Your man picked that out for you, didn't he?" Vissa tittered at that, and Treneth chortled.

"Yes," I said, because it was far safer to blame Rhaim than to admit that his spider had.

But after that, there was no denying I knew Rhaim—especially when we took a break and I had to explain all the items in my basket.

"It's like a Darkest Day morning in here!" Vissa said, going through everything that'd been given me, laying them out on the already-dry sheet we'd spread out upon.

We had Darkest Day celebrations in our chambers every year, my family and I. All I'd known as a child was that it was the day we all got presents, and it'd taken an embarrassingly long time for me to understand why the day was called that, especially because it was only when one of my tutors explained it.

But when I never saw the sunrise, the sunset, or the moon at night, how could I know that there was one night that was longer than any other each year?

It wasn't really until after the Deathless appeared that morning that the name made sense to me. By the time my father's men had retaken the room from them, and come to unlock my door—when they wouldn't let me see my mother, but it was clear that there was nothing left of her, and whatever presents she had meant to give me, and all of mine for her, had been rudely shoveled into the fire. Then I remember thinking, *Yes, this day is dark.*

"So you're the mage's woman?" Treneth asked with a squint. I got the impression she might have asked the question more than once already, as I blinked back to attention.

"I am not," I said, definitively. "I'm his friend. We travel together." And I was *here*, now, not trapped in chambers. I took several deep breaths, pushing away my intrusive memories.

"*Travel*," Vissa said, with the same tone she'd used for Jelena's "sleeping" earlier. She uncorked the glass and scented its contents. "Amber!" she crowed, taking a sip, before handing it over.

I gulped it, same as she had, and then sputtered as it burned. "Gah—"

"That's how you know it's good," Jelena informed me, taking the bottle from my hand and taking a swig.

"Come on, come on," Treneth muttered. I thought she was waiting for her turn with the bottle, but she was talking to the lid of the jar of preserves instead, and she grinned when she caught me watching her. "I'm sure Old Woman Crassby gave you the good stuff, from the drought two years back—made all the plums sweeter."

"Now that I know, I hope so," I told her, giving her a tentative smile as she finally pried the lid off.

We passed it around, dipping in chunks of bread we'd ripped from the loaf. It was warm, and a breeze had sprung up, which cheered the girls because the drying would go faster. The sound of the river was lovely, I was pleasantly exhausted, and soon my stomach was full.

I lay down and threw an arm across my eyes, basking in the sunlight.

This was what getting to live a life was like.

This was what it meant to be free.

"So tell us about him," Jelena asked, flopping onto her stomach beside me.

"And your *travels*," Vissa pressed.

I pushed myself up on one arm. "I'd rather not."

A bird swooped down, eyeing the crumbs of bread that were left and then eyeing me in turn. And suddenly, my mood, which had felt so expansive prior, shrank into a sliver of a shadow.

Every bird we'd passed on the way here, every insect, every fish that'd swam by—Rhaim could control.

I'd never truly been alone—and nowhere near as free as I desired.

He'd just let me think I'd been, for a bit.

No one noticed the changing of my mood, except for perhaps Jelena.

"He's very mean," I said, wondering if the bird would report that back directly. "He lets me think I'm in charge of things, when really I'm not. And he pretends—" I went on, but Treneth swung a hand out, and the bird flew away before I could finish.

He pretends that he could care for me, though we both know that he doesn't.

Jelena frowned on my behalf, as I looked toward her. "Can you help me get some pants?"

Her eyebrows shot up. "Like the trader girls?"

"Yes?" I guessed, and she nodded.

"Of course."

Jelena took me back to the tavern late that afternoon, just before dark. The things that had been given to me were distributed between all the other girls, and my basket now held just as many linens to return as theirs all did. Jelena and I went in the side door, catching a surprised Pella in the kitchen.

"There you are!" she exclaimed in surprise at me. "Go to your room, and I'll bring you some food—I was looking all over for you!"

Pella, maybe. But... "Was he looking for me?" I asked. Had Rhaim even bothered to pretend to be worried about my absence? He'd known exactly where I was the entire time.

She blinked. "Should he have been?"

I shook my head and the thought away, following Jelena up the stairs—she brought me to my door. "My older brother is about your size and away. I can steal some of his pants; I think they'll fit you."

"Thank you. Wait a moment?" I asked her, going into my room, and leaving the door open behind me. I took off Rhaim's cloak and hung it on the bed's headboard in my room—and then reached for the first of Finx's dresses, shimmying it off.

Jelena stared. "Lirane?"

"For you," I said, handing it to her. I didn't have coins to offer her, but I did have this—and she and I were similar sizes as well. Plus, the silk had a bit of stretch.

"I couldn't possibly," she said, refusing to take it.

"You must," I said. She put the basket she held down and tentatively took it. "It's spider silk," I explained. "And the spider's a friend. He'd be mad at me if I didn't give it to you in trade for the pants."

"Spider silk?" she whispered, petting the dress, before trying to hand it back again. "Lirane, this is finer than anything else I'll ever own."

I wasn't sure how to answer that as we stared one another down. I knew there was an awkward gulf between our realities, one that either one of us could've easily fallen into. Then I thought of what I hoped was the right thing to say. "I'm glad it's yours now. I had a very fine day. Thank you for including me."

The edges of her lips quirked up in a smile. "You do seem rather angry. You'd make a good laundry maid."

I laughed. "Thank you for that, too."

Jelena petted the silk with another stroke. "I am going to make so much money with this dress until the traders come to town again. You have no idea."

"You're right, I don't," I agreed with her.

She giggled, and then sobered. "Lirane—I'm very sorry."

A stone of dread dropped in my belly. "For what?" Were Vethys's people around the corner? Or had Rhaim paid her to be my friend?

"Last night. When your man got you both rooms—I thought you were his distant cousin, or a ward. If I had known you were his lady, I might not have tried so hard...although truth be told, that probably wouldn't have stopped me." She shrugged a shoulder, as she winced with honesty. "He had coin, and I had hopes."

And that was the one way in which we were both very much alike, despite having been born to different stations. "Some days I am made of nothing but hope—so I have no need of your apology," I told her, and she smiled. "Also, please believe me—I am not his lady. His time is his own."

Pella reached the top of the stairs, carrying a tray of food. She stopped at a different room down the hall to drop off dinner, but spotted Jelena. "Girl, stop bothering the guests. Get back to work!" Jelena shoved the dress into the linen basket as she picked it up. I jumped back into my room and pulled the cloak back on.

"Pants?" I asked her quickly.

"Tomorrow!" she promised, and sprinted off, then Pella was there, and it was my turn for dinner.

Pella balanced her tray on her hip and handed me two bowls of some sort of stew, then tucked a loaf of bread under one of my elbows and a bottle of wine under the other. "Have a nice night!" she said before heading down the hall.

I stood in front of Rhaim's door, and kicked it sullenly. "I know you're in there."

"How can you be sure?" he asked from inside, and then opened the door. He took one of the bowls from me and then pulled the door wider. "Would you like to eat in here again tonight, or should we divide the bread and wine in the hall?" I inhaled deeply and walked in as answer. "Look, I've even managed a chair for you," he said, gesturing to one that sat opposite him.

"And now I feel like I'm back at court again," I said, taking it, after managing to set my bowl and bread down without dropping the wine bottle. He produced a knife from somewhere on his person and wiggled out the cork.

We ate in silence for a time, him sitting again on his bed across from me. "How was the rest of your day?" I asked, when I was nearly through.

"There's now a massive migration of ticks, abandoning their furry friends and heading due east, because I didn't know what else to do with them."

I blinked, the stew-soaked bread I'd been about to put in my mouth hovering. "Couldn't you have fed them to spiders?"

"And get the spiders used to sheep's blood? Nothing good can come of that." His face was stern for a moment, and then he cracked a smile.

"Bah," I said, and finished my bite.

"And your day?" he asked, pushing his bowl aside.

"Lovely. I ate jam on a riverbank—which I know you know."

He waved a dismissive hand between us. "I checked in once or twice."

"Somehow I doubt that."

Rhaim chuckled darkly. "Fine. I had several birds, three lizards, and two crickets watching you. Is that what you'd like to hear?"

I flushed. "No."

He crossed his hands above his bowl, and gazed at me across his knuckles. "You are too precious to me to fully abandon, moth. Plus—despite the kindness of your new friends, no place is truly safe."

I had been hoping he'd say as much, because it was the only excuse he had for spying on me continually. I tilted my chin slightly. "If that's true...then you had better train me."

Rhaim closed his eyes and sighed. "No."

I waited quite some time for his eyes to open again, and the second they did I repeated him. "No? No for now—or no forever?" This time I couldn't help but sound panicked—and angry.

"Just no," he said simply in return.

I had heard a lifetime of *no*s coming out from mages' mouths, and hearing it now from him was every bit as infuriating as all of theirs had been. "Why not?" I protested. "Surely you're not too tired to—" My voice drifted as I realized I didn't even fully know what I was asking for—and he knew that.

"Too tired to what, moth?" he asked, his expression calmly shifting as he studied me. "After all, I wouldn't want you to think that I was mean."

I blanched. "So you were listening!"

"Not all the time," he said, shrugging lightly. "But I did hear that."

I turned an even brighter shade of red, underneath where the sun had kissed me. “If I had thought you had feelings to hurt, I would’ve been quieter.”

He snorted. “When you actually hurt my feelings, you’ll know, moth. But go back to your room now. I’m tired, and I have another exciting day of delousing livestock to look forward to tomorrow.”

I stood, embarrassed, picked up my bowl, and reached for the wine bottle. He swatted my hand away. “This stays with me,” he said, picking it up and almost draining it dry. “Sleep well, moth,” he told my retreating form, and I didn’t answer him, as I went back to my room across the hall, dismissed.

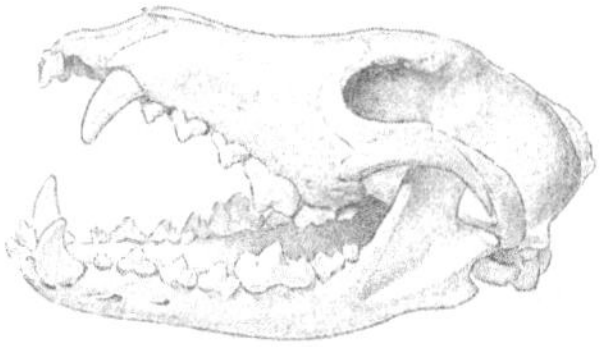

9

RHAIM

Had it been disappointing discovering that my moth thought all I did was hurt her?

Yes.

But I already knew as much from reading her journal, so I shouldn't have been surprised.

It hadn't stopped her from asking to be trained twice now, though. And while I'd dismissed her out of hand both times, seeing as I would prefer to give any interaction with her my full concentration, rather than my mind being pieced out around the countryside and full of concerns about my castle, I'd seen her look of panic, at thinking that I might stop.

I polished off the bottle of wine and wiped my lips with the back of one hand.

Did she really want to continue?

And even if she did—should I let her? Damnable Sibyi had made several good points earlier, which I had decided to hate him for ever since.

I'd only warned Lisane that becoming a mage would render her barren once—that fact probably bore repeating. And if she did manage to earn her mage-mark—without bursting into flames prior—there was the whole matter of the rest of her life. She would heal more quickly and become stronger, but her aging would slow. People she loved would wither and die. Some mages went mad sheerly from living for too long, and actively sought out ways to hasten their demise.

And I still needed to explain a mage's Ascension to her, now that—*if*—it might actually happen. As bad as she'd thought she'd been hurt already, I was sure none of it compared to the feeling of getting branded by fate itself. The pain of receiving my mage-mark—I'd felt it all the way through my soul.

But before discussing any of that...I needed to judge her intent.

My fear was that she saw magical training only as a means to an end. I knew she was horrified at the thought of going back to women's chambers. What if she thought the only way to stay out of them was to let me keep hurting her?

I didn't feel as if it were something I could ask her, without also accidentally putting the idea inside her mind.

I kicked off my boots and stretched out on the bed, glad I'd taken the opportunity earlier at my castle to bathe so I didn't stink like ten different kinds of goat. The wine bottle's glass filtered and diffracted the dim lamp light, sending its beam in all the wrong directions, and I realized it was like there was also a glass between Lisane and I.

I would say one thing, and she would hear another. I would command her, and she would disobey me. I would show her a kindness, and she would rather feel a palm.

I had met creatures like her before—not quite reptile, but not quite mammal, either—that curled to wrap in scales at the slightest touch. Them, I could convince of my well-meaning, but her?

I did not know.

And every day around her it felt like she wrapped herself in longer spikes.

She had been happy for a time though, out with the other women. I'd seen it. I knew she had happiness in her.

Just perhaps not with me.

Knowing that...was it fair to keep her?

Even if she thought I should?

I was thinking on that when I heard the sound of the wall outside my room being hit with stones.

A mage would've likely portaled closer, and a man would've come in to threaten me, so I already had an idea what I'd be dealing with by the time I got outside and walked around the tavern's edge.

Sure enough, there were three children there, a tall boy, a small girl, and in between them was the boy I'd paid a coin to yesterday.

"It's dark—why are you lot out?" I asked, though I already knew what he held inside his hands.

"My pet's not well, mage-sir," the tallest one said. The boy I'd paid a coin to nudged him forward, and he took a nervous step, holding cupped hands out to me. I cleared the distance between us and knelt down. He was holding a skinny black rat with a stump of a tail. I reached in, and let it sniff my finger. "His name's Ratty, sir, and he's always been my pet. Can you fix him?"

I put my hands around the boy's until he released the rat to me and concentrated. Rats could be wise, even if they only had short lives. He told me of lint in pockets, warm pillows, and a belly full of crumbs and cheese. "He's not sick, he's just very, very old," I told the child. "Impressively so, actually.

You gave him a good life. He enjoyed it very much, but he will die soon."

The boy's upper lip wavered, and the girl began to cry.

"Isn't there anything you can do?" the tavern boy asked me earnestly.

"I'm sorry." I held the rat in the palm of one hand and carefully stroked his fur. "All things must die, eventually."

The little girl looked me up and down. "How old are you?"

"Eight hundred and thirty-four. But I am as my magic made me."

"And you can't magic him?" the tavern boy pressed.

"Even I cannot deny death. And there will come a time when it will come for me, too." I cast a glance up to the tavern's second floor, where Lisane was now sleeping across the hall from my room.

The tallest boy came up and scooped Ratty back into his own hands. I stood again.

"You know what I can do, however," I told the three of them. "You have taken such good care of Ratty—let us let him help pick you out his successor."

Ratty the Rat wouldn't actually care—he would die in his sleep in a few days—but the child didn't need to know that, and if he thought his own pet had passed along his crown, it would lessen the blow. And given as good of care as Ratty had gotten, I wouldn't feel bad leaving a new rat with the boy.

"Where did you find him?" I asked. "A barn, a field, or a trash heap?"

"Behind Mister Wather's barn," he said solemnly.

"Let's start there then. Show me the way," I said, sweeping an arm out to pull along the others.

10

LISANE

It was just barely possible that Rhaim was truly doing me a favor—because the second I made it back to my room, took off my cloak, and crawled into bed, sleep was coming for me. My hips and legs were still sore from the horse, and now my arms and back were sore from beating laundry. I didn't even manage to turn off my lamp; I just cast an arm across my face after lying down and I was out...until a strange sound woke me.

I blinked, even stiffer now than I had been before, wiping a hand across my eyes and some drool from the corner of my lips—and I heard the sound again.

A manly grunt, and a breathy groan.

I sat up in bed quickly, as the sounds repeated, along with a woman's soft, "Oh, yes."

I had a feeling I knew what they were from...but I didn't know who was making them.

I heard another grunt, a wet smack, and a sigh.

It felt wrong listening in—*and undeniably titillating*—until I considered who it could be.

I had relinquished all claims to Rhaim earlier on in the day, several times—and I had meant it—hadn't I?

I'd thought so at the time.

But now, thinking of him making the sounds I was hearing through the wall—pleased sounds, speeding up, in louder volume—there wasn't an appropriate word I could use for it. Anger wasn't hot enough, and betrayal not as fierce. I knew I had no right to either feeling, but that didn't stop a hot tide of acid from rising up inside my throat.

I got up from my bed quietly, opened the door as softly as I could, and then walked across the hall, my clouded thoughts ringing in my ears just as loud as the activities I heard—I tried for Rhaim's door without knocking, because I wanted to startle him—

His door swung open, unlocked, because there was nothing in the room to steal.

He was someplace else.

Possibly *with* someone else.

And as angry as I was at him, almost all of the time, the thought of it made me want to retch.

I closed his door and leaned upon it as the sounds reached a crescendo, both of the people involved in making them sounding intensely satisfied, until a girl's voice called out repeatedly, her pleasure counterpointed by a man's rough, low grunts. I clutched an impotent fist to my chest, ready to scream, when I finally heard their conversation.

"Wait a bit, girl, and we can go again—"

I didn't know who it was...but it wasn't Rhaim.

It felt like I could breathe again.

"And were you going to pay me twice as much?" asked a woman with a familiar voice. The man groaned, and the woman laughed lightly. "Maybe tomorrow, then."

"If only I could pay you instead of Pella," he complained.

"If you stiff her for lodging, I won't let you stiff me," the woman said and laughed again. Then the door they were behind opened revealing Jelena, dressed in the spider-silk dress I had given her. She grinned when she spotted me, and held up two coins for show, then patted the side of her new dress, and mouthed the words, "Thank you!"

I waved haplessly and went back into my room to throw myself upon the bed, content to bunk down with my idiocy.

When I woke up the next morning, my mind was made up, and my mood was clear. The dining room of the tavern was empty again, and I could hear the bleating of all sorts of creatures just outside.

"Pella?" I asked, when the woman came to serve me. "Where does Jelena live?"

She made a face. "Small cottage near the river's edge of town."

"Could you be more descriptive?"

"Used to be red," she said, then made a tiny box with her hands. "*Very* small. Why?"

"No reason!" I said, grabbing the rolls on my plate before heading out.

This time I took the kitchen exit and snuck out quietly. I was sure Rhaim would see me through some beast's eyes soon enough, but that was all right, as long as none of the rest of the townspeople spotted me.

I went toward where I thought the river was, and then when I got there, wound around the side of it, going from place to place, until I found a small living place, practically wedged in between two bigger buildings, and it was a kind of dirty maroon color. I knocked on its door, and when no one answered in a reasonable amount of time, I knocked again, harder.

“What is it?” shouted someone from inside. “No one’s home!”

“Jelena?” I asked—then I heard wood scrape wood as a small viewport inside the door opened, and Jelena peered out.

“Lirane? Why are you here?”

I held up the two rolls. “Can I tell you inside? I brought food.”

Jelena opened up a series of levers inside the door and let me in. If I had thought Rhaim’s and my rooms at the tavern were small, Jelena’s abode made me adjust my expectations. There was a bed along one wall, a cramped stove at the back, and very few other belongings. A carved horse, a few pots, and a trunk, and she was wearing a plain linen gown with light soot stains on it.

I offered the roll over to her, while she continued to look at me strangely. “Are you here for the pants?”

“Yes,” I said, although I’d completely forgotten about them with all of my other plans.

She nodded, put the roll in her mouth, and opened up the trunk to go through things. My spider-silk dress was folded neatly on top. When she reached the right item she made a sound and pulled it out.

“Will these fit you?” she asked, as I took them and measured them against my hips.

“I think so.”

“Then they’re yours. They were my brother’s, but he’s not here right now—he’ll be back again in a few months, when the traders return.” I nodded like that meant something to me, although I had no idea where there’d be room for another person in here with her. “Next time they leave, I’m going with them,” she said. “With the money I’ve been saving and your dress, I think they’ll take me.”

“Take you...where?”

“Away from here. Like you.” She sat down on the closed trunk and hugged herself. “I want to see the world. And maybe find myself a nobleman. I could be like a high-born lady and someone could feed me fruit all day.” I reacted with horror at the thought, but she thought I was mocking her hopes. She rolled her eyes and gave me a silly grin, shrugging. “Fine, probably not, but who can say?”

"Who indeed," I made myself say kindly, before sitting on the edge of her bed. "I can give you two more dresses, if you can also find me a shirt and teach me."

Her mouth fell into a startled O. "The—that's—" she stuttered as I stood up, tossing Rhaim's cloak off. At least now I wasn't unnerved by casual nudity—I started shimmying the dresses off, at the same moment she began to take me seriously, diving into the trunk for extra clothing.

She flung a shirt at me. It was too big, so I tucked in one side and then the other, into the top of the pants, making a V of the neckline, before pulling the cloak back on. When I was finished, she was holding a dress in each hand, while she gawked. "Teach you what?" she asked.

"How to be like you." I squatted in front of her in the pants, finding it easier with no skirt to manage. *Men had been cheating with their clothing all this time.*

"What can you possibly mean?"

"The things you do at night. I want to know what they are. No funny jokes or strange meanings, like Vissa had yesterday—just the truth."

Jelena groaned and rolled her eyes. "A girl as pretty as you, Lirane, you don't even need to try—any number of men would show you."

I sat back on the edge of her bed. "I do not want any number of men. I only need the one."

Her eyes widened in understanding. "So it's like that, is it?" she asked with a cunning nod.

"It is."

She bit her lip and gave me a slightly feral smile. "And can I pierce your ears?"

I grinned back at her. "Absolutely."

Learning did not take all morning—for as mysterious as books and my mother had made things sound, the mechanics seemed easy enough.

So after that we went and found Treneth, and after Jelena explained my situation, she chimed in with her opinions.

"You can't just go in there and offer yourself up to him." I had rather been planning on doing just that. I wanted him to teach me, this seemed the most expedient course. "You should give him some secrets to solve," she said, with an expansive gesture, and then she saw my pants. "And those certainly aren't helping."

And when we caught up with Vissa, she stared me down. "You're joking."

"I'm not."

She grunted and said, "Wait here."

She ran back into her house—it was almost as big as the tavern—and when she returned she had a small fabric bundle in her hands, which she unfolded carefully to reveal what looked like a gleaming bone splinter.

"What is that?" I wondered.

"A shard of unicorn horn." I only knew of them from bridal ceremonies—huge, full-sized ones, ivory horns twisting to a tip, longer than my arms were. Vissa handed it over to Jelena, who sighed, and picked it up. The gleam on the bone went away, becoming dull. Vissa then offered it over to me—and I remembered Rhaim's head between my legs.

I had nothing to lose though, here—I picked up the shard, and it began shining.

Vissa laughed at that, took it, and folded it back up. "Every month or two I find another little girl to let hold it, then I'm careful to wrap it up in fabric until it's time to show my mother. When my mother bought it from the trader, she never asked if I needed to touch it, or just be near it—and she's afraid to touch it herself, in front of me, because then I'd know how I was born."

"Our mothers had much in common then," I said. "What would she do to you if she found it dull?"

"She'd make me get married," Vissa said, then made a sound like a cat with a hairball. Treneth and Jelena laughed at this, and I laughed right along with them.

I made sure not to return to the tavern before nightfall well after Jelena was done with me and had wished me good luck.

And then I walked in the front, with Rhaim's cloak pulled around me. When I didn't see him downstairs, I went up and quietly knocked on his door.

"Come in," he said from the inside. He was sitting in the chair, there was food atop his table, and in one hand he held a book.

I forgot most of my plan at that point.

"Where did you get the book from?"

"I portaled to the castle, to check in on things. Repairs are going apace, and Finx said to tell you hello."

I wondered what Finx would think of me now, now that I'd given three of his pretty dresses away.

"Did you want to eat?" Rhaim asked, gesturing at the place setting across from him.

I hadn't eaten anything since my roll early in the morning—but if I paused to eat, I'd lose my nerve, so I shook my head. "No. I wish to train."

Rhaim groaned at that. "I have spent another day immersed in the needs of both animals and humans, moth. You got to have fun with your friends while I worked. I would like to relax now."

I stood stiffly near the door, measuring him. "You think you can content me with a peasant's life?"

He gave me a glare. "A peasant's life? Is there any true dirt under your nails? You want for nothing."

"Nothing, except for what I have always longed for."

Rhaim closed his book and turned his chair towards me. "The people here treat you like a queen."

I lifted my chin. "I could've already been a queen, had I gone quietly with Vethys." His eyes narrowed thoughtfully as I continued. "I want to be a mage."

"Moth," he began, making it a sigh as I started reaching for the clasps of the cloak I wore and letting it fall open. "Why are you dressed entirely like a boy?" he asked next.

My lips pulled into a line. I was determined, but this wasn't going easily. "I had to trade my clothes for knowledge."

One of his eyebrows arched high. "That makes it sound like there are someone's eyes I should pop."

"I know you watched me today, Rhaim." I folded his cloak up in my arms and set it down.

"I do not deny it." And he was watching me now, like a curious cat.

"Then you know exactly where I was, and who I was with."

"The girls who painted your lips with berries and hooped metal through your earlobes."

I nodded. "Yes. They explained many things to me."

"Did they now?" he said, his voice rich with the sarcasm I was accustomed to from him.

"They did." I swallowed and stiffened my spine. "You called me your consort yesterday, to the townspeople. I am ready to claim that title, if it comes with training."

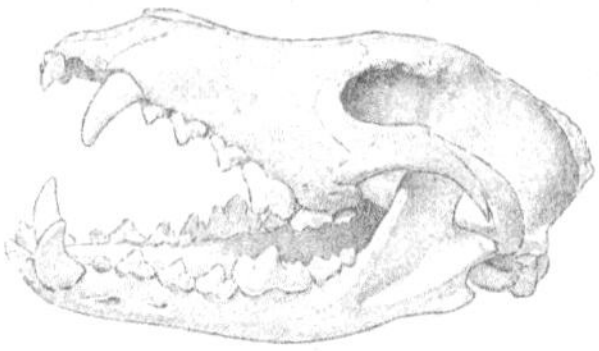

11

RHAIM

I had kept a few eyes on Lisane at all times throughout the day—a bird here, a mouse there, just enough for me to know what was happening with her, but I couldn't claim to have been paying close attention, as busy as I was treating farmers' livestock at the well.

I knew she was whole, I knew she was safe, and I'd caught her smiling, again. Happier without me—and also without magic in her life.

"Moth," I began, ready to talk some sense into her. We needed to have a real conversation, and while I would've rather it happen a few days from now, if she was going to push my hand...

Then I watched her get down on her hands and knees and all of my wisdom left me.

"You once had me crawl to you like a cat," she said, beginning to do so. Her hair swung freely, as the shirt she'd wrapped on opened slightly, showing me the soft inner curves of her breasts. "If that is what you want—if that is what it takes," she said, making her way forward with each phrase.

"Lisane," I warned, but I didn't stop her. Her berry-stained lips were parted, her brow furrowed in familiar concentration, and I knew if she had any magic in her at the moment that she would be using it on me. She almost met my knees and changed from crawling to kneeling.

"I want you to train me, Rhaim. And I know you want that too." She rose up, same as I had in the tub with her, her head between my thighs, and kept her amber eyes on mine, even as her fingers went for the leather laces of my breeches.

I was painfully aware of both her proximity and the depths to which indulging her was a bad idea, but the lower her hands worked, her fingertips tracing on the outside of my leathers, the harder my fat cock swelled beneath them. "I do not want to hurt you, moth. And I heard you yesterday—you do not wish me to be mean to you."

She quickly shook her head and pouted. "You didn't understand me. You're mean to me when you *don't* train me. When you *don't* let me make up my own mind. When you think you know what's better for me than I do."

If I even believed that for a second, I had no time to question it, wondering what it was she planned to do next—if her bravery would exhaust itself, and I would have to take myself in hand again.

But then she reached into my leathers, pushing them aside, and for a moment, if she had asked me for the moon, I would have found a way to grab it for her. Her delicate fingers wrapped around my dark, heavy shaft, and her cheeks blushed more pink than the stain she'd placed upon them, as she pulled me out, gently stroking back my sheath—and then she saw the fearsome ring I'd had pierced through the tip of my cock and stopped with a gasp. She was breathing so hard I could feel it against my head, as eager drops of clear fluid beaded from my tip around the metal. She glanced from me to my cock and back again.

"What?" I asked her coolly, knowing full well how annoying it was. She briefly frowned up at me, uncertainty warring with pride in her expression. Her little pink tongue thoughtfully licked her lips before she leaned in to lap at my precum, gliding against the cool metal and my hot flesh, tasting me carefully, like any gift from me might poison her. Then, finding me agreeable, she carefully kissed my tip with her soft closed lips, and I nearly lifted out of my chair.

I swallowed an inchoate sound, longing to take myself in hand and smear myself against her lips, to paint them with my own fluid instead of berries, but I managed to restrain myself and wait, as her small mouth opened up and she took my head inside, with the light teeth of an inexperienced girl.

She held it there, gently sucking, running her tongue against the bottom of my head and across my slit, pushing the metal I'd set into myself back and forth, letting it click against her teeth, before opening her eyes to look up, trying to determine if she'd elicited the response from me she wanted.

If what she wanted was to inflame me with crude desires for her, then yes, that was working—but I showed her nothing other than my obvious arousal, watching her impassively, and as her enthusiasm faded, she sat back and let me go, looking peeved.

"Is that all?" I asked her, imperiously.

Her jaw clenched as her eyes narrowed. "Don't be difficult."

I laughed harshly. "I am rather the opposite, right now," I said, and reached down to replace myself inside my leathers, but her hands swatted me away.

"I know the truth of things, Rhaim—and I didn't even need to read your journal."

"The truth, eh? And what is that, little moth?" I asked her, in a tone of disregard. The truth was, I wanted her to want me, not just to want things from me...although I knew the longer this charade went on, the less I would care about her intent.

"I know that you like it," she said slowly, before gathering speed and volume, continuing to push my hands back. "And I know that you're not scared of hurting me—you're scared of liking it too much."

I let one half of a cruel smile rock up. "Is that so?"

She fought with me for another moment, then gave up. "It is!" Her hands curled into fists of frustration as she sank down. "I know you are a monster, Rhaim! I've *seen* him! I—"

I lunged out and caught her lower jaw in one hand, pushing my thumb into her mouth against her tongue, before pulling her up with it, like I had caught a mermaid with a hook. Her eyes went wide. She couldn't speak, and her hands scrabbled at my thighs for purchase.

"You think you've met him, have you?" I asked her, knowing she couldn't answer. She didn't know the truth of things—she probably thought my beast was totally *other.*

She had no idea that *he* was also *me.*

"Open. Up," I said, shaking her jaw, and taking myself in hand.

Her eyes went wide, but she did as she was told, breathing roughly over the back of my hand, her whole body tense with...anticipation?

Fear?

I didn't know.

I wasn't sure I cared.

"Do not bite me," I warned, then slid my hand back to grab a fistful of her hair, bringing her mouth forward to plunge her mouth around my cock as my other hand aimed it for her, ramming in as much of me as she could take.

She made a muffled sound and her fingers clenched into my leathers. I could feel the way the bend of her throat held me, as the muscles there quivered and twitched, her tongue pressed against my cock's belly, her mouth enveloping me in soft, wet heat.

Somewhere in my laboratory, there was the exceedingly brief journal of a mage whose power was bringing up other people's memories. He'd been murdered rather quickly after helping someone to remember the wrong thing, not long after he'd gotten his mage-mark.

But if he lived now, and Lisane left me, I would've sought him out, just to get the chance to relive this moment: the quiet, needy, frightened noises she was still making, the way her hair's caress felt against my sack, and the beauty of her utter servitude, now that I was finally getting to experience it.

A wild thought rose in me, unbidden: *we liked her on her knees.*

So I held her there for long enough to memorize the way it felt as best I could, and then I let her go.

My little moth sagged back and down, onto all fours, gasping for air, thoughtlessly drooling onto the scuffed wooden floor.

I stroked myself at the sight of her. If I thought I ached any prior night, no—this was actual agony. Her mouth and throat had been warm and tight, and now here I was, exposed to the air and cold, without her lips wrapped around me, stiff as wood from a kaorak tree, and I needed to come more than I'd ever needed anything.

More than magic.

More than love.

She caught her breath and slowly rocked her head back to look up at me. I expected to see a world of betrayal or pain inside her copper eyes, but instead there was a dangerous ferocity, her continual stubbornness mixed with something wild and hungry.

My moth brought the back of her hand up to wipe the spittle from her mouth. "Did you hope I would grow gills?"

I snorted. "Surely I have already hurt you enough tonight to put magic inside of you." It was the last warning I would give her.

I watched her swallow and lick her swelling lips, still looking utterly determined, and then she rose up to pad one palm against each of my thighs like a large and compliant cat. "I would like to be hurt more, sir."

I sucked in air, suddenly so hard it stole my breath, and instantly reached to take my shirt off.

12

LISANE

I didn't know what I was asking for—I just knew I wanted *it*—and as Rhaim took his shirt off for me, I knew that *it* was coming.

I hadn't seen him naked since I'd caught him near his tub, about to bathe, when he'd been wounded and also angry at me. But now I had a chance to appreciate the build of his body, the way he was covered in rippling muscles, faint scars, and a dusting of black hair—and his mage-mark was in the same place as where I'd touched it on his beast.

It'd been clear his beast had wanted me then—and it was clear *he* wanted me now.

"Give me your hand," he commanded, once his shirt was tossed aside.

I did as I was told, and he used it to wrap himself, then taking it up and down his length in long, smooth strokes, before letting go so that I was on my own. I kept going, and more of that strange fluid Jelena had warned me about wept out of him, around the thick piece of metal he wore that I couldn't quite believe was there—especially after getting my own ears pierced today. His eyes were dark on mine, his breathing rough, and his cock tugged against my palm like it was a separate creature. "Do whatever you like, until I give you direction," he told me.

I was scared of this shift between us, even though I wanted more. "What do you like best?" I asked.

"You are a mage," he said, sinking one hand again to circle himself at his base. "Experiment and find out."

His cock was warm, hard on the whole, but soft on the outside, and I couldn't fully wrap my fingers around it. It was wrapped in a sheath that moved as my hand did, and it was over three palm widths long.

"What if what *I* like best is to bite you?" I asked while stroking.

His lips curved in a fearless smile. "Then your training will be abrupt."

I rolled my eyes. When Jelena and the other girls had told me how this would go, I had felt confident I could manage it, until here and now—it sounded like the men in town were much more pliable than Rhaim. And none of the girls had mentioned anything about secret jewelry.

I should've known he wouldn't make things easy for me.

But I still wanted what he had. He was the key to my magical future. *And?* I wanted to know where this would lead. When I was brave enough to look up at him again, the way he was watching me was as hot as his hand or his whip had ever been.

So I brought my lips to his tip again and licked away more of the clear fluid there. Strange that I had never kissed his lips, nor he mine, and yet now we'd both tasted each other. And as my tongue stroked against him, he gave a settling sigh.

I took his length into both hands and kept going, licking at him with the broad part of my tongue, from side to side, as his jewelry permitted.

"Suck on me, moth," he instructed, and I nodded quickly, rising up, taking his head into my mouth again. He made another satisfied sound once I was there, and I remembered the noises he'd made between my thighs, pleasured by my pleasure, and now I understood—the space between my legs ached, my nipples were tight and hard—and I moaned back at him, for him, for myself, as I tried to take him deeper.

He groaned at that, arching back in the chair, using the hand he had on himself to push himself down for me, and when I looked up, I saw his jaw dropped, and his dangerously bright eyes half-lidded. “Less teeth, vicious moth,” he said, with a chuckle.

That was a thing Jelena had warned me about. I pulled off of him. “Sorry,” I said. My jaw felt wide, my lips stretched, and...I wished I still had a dress on, because I wanted to crawl up into his lap and let him take me. I had no idea how there would be room for the part of him I sucked on to fit inside myself, metal and all, and yet I knew with all my being that I wanted it there.

“Don’t be. You of all people should understand the value of practice.” His words were kind, but he sounded amused. I squinted up at him.

“Do you really want me practicing magic on your cock?” I asked.

He outright laughed before answering. “It has a magic all its own, little moth, that I am eager to show you.” Then he used his circling hand to push himself down again.

I took the hint and brought my lips to him once more, but stopped. “What does it feel like when I taste you?”

“Good.”

My cheeks went red and my resolve fluttered. "Just good?" I asked because that didn't sound "good" enough to me.

He reached forward, I thought to grab me again and choke me, but all he did was push my hair back from my shoulder—to make it easier for him to watch. "It feels like you are painting me with welcome fire."

That...was better. And I honestly couldn't have explained how I'd felt when he had done the same thing to me. I took his head back in my mouth, cupped my lips around my teeth, and slid on and off of him while sucking, and stroking with my two hands, as he rocked back and moaned.

"Yes, moth. Like that," he said.

I made a sound against him, angling my head so I could fit more of him in my mouth.

"Faster with your hands," he urged, briefly taking mine inside his free one, so I would know the speed he wanted. He started to breathe harder, and it did feel like I was doing magic of a sort as I pulled reactions from him, breath and groans and moans, as his hips arched up, bucking him into my throat. I grunted at that, trying to manage to take him and do what he wanted, while needing him utterly.

I wanted to make him feel like he had me—and then I wanted to have my turn feeling like that again, too.

"Moth," he warned, and I sank as low as I could on him, hitting my lips with my hands as I stroked him. "Moth," he said again, and groaned, running a hand into my hair to grab it again, I thought to hold me to his satisfaction, but instead he roughly pushed me back, his metal ring clacking against my teeth.

I made a frustrated sound without thinking. I didn't know what I had done wrong—I was breathing as hard as he was—but his hand in my hair was tight, and even though I left my mouth open, he wouldn't push himself back in.

Instead, he stared down the plane of his stomach at me as he used his other hand to stroke himself, then rocked back, hissing, as his hips shifted forward, and he said, "Fuck, moth—*fuck,*" while holding onto the end of himself, then growled as the muscles of his stomach clenched in pulsing synchrony as his cock jerked. "*Fuck,*" he said again, in a guttural tone, as another spasm rolled through him, and then a third.

Then he inhaled deeply, and released his hand from my hair, his eyes dark on mine, his own jaw slightly dropped, as he moved his hand away from his cock. I followed it with my eyes, knowing what had happened, at least in theory, and moved to catch his wrist and bring it forward.

His palm was covered in milky white fluid, more opaque than the waters of his healing bath, just like Jelena had sworn there'd be—and I was still on all fours, like a cat. I brought his hand toward me, licked at it like cream, and immediately made a face. Its taste was salty, strange, and unexpected.

Rhaim watched me, catching his breath, and then he laughed. "Did your friends lie and tell you that it was going to taste good?"

"No," I said, shaking my head—and as he tried to take his hand away from me, I fought him. "Let me finish what I started," I said, and brought his palm down for me to lick again. Jelena had said it was very important to swallow, though Treneth and Vissa disagreed—but I knew from the look Rhaim was giving me now, how his thighs tensed and his nostrils flared, that I had made the right decision. He watched me, his chest heaving.

"Do not grant me this power over you, Lisane," he whispered, when I was almost through.

"Why not?" I asked, darting my tongue between his fingers, chasing every drop.

"Because I am not worthy of it." His eyes were dark and his expression solemn.

Was that what he truly thought? *Why?* I sat back on my heels in front of him once his hand was clean. "If you don't hurt me to train me, who will?"

"The girls who pierced your ears, perhaps," he said, frowning, pushing himself roughly back into his leather breeches to fasten his laces.

"I don't want them, Rhaim. They know nothing of magic." I felt bereft and was starting to panic. Had everything up to this point been wasted? Did he truly feel nothing toward me? I bowed my head because I couldn't bear to watch my rejection. "I want you, sir. Please."

I waited with bated breath, still able to taste him, and the moment between us stretched overly long. I was sure that I had played some part of my role in error and missed something that all other girls knew but me.

And then he took a deep inhale, that seemed to drag part of my soul in with it.

"I have tamed enough beasts today, moth," he said, quietly. My shoulders sank, thinking all was lost until he continued. "But tomorrow, while I work, go buy the longest, softest rope you can find, and the heaviest cane you think you can take."

I replayed what he'd said in my head until I believed it and looked up. "Do you promise it? No matter what you hear from birds?"

"No matter what I hear from birds," he repeated. "I promise, little moth. Nothing will stop me." I had the briefest moment to wonder if that was worrisome as he offered down his unlicked hand. I took it and let him help me rise. “Now go to sleep,” he said, jerking his chin toward his door. “I would like to finish my book.”

My heart started beating in my throat, already terrified I’d get exactly what I’d wanted. “Good-night then, All-Beast,” I said, picking his cloak up off the floor.

“Moth,” he said, casually dipping his head, and I left him alone.

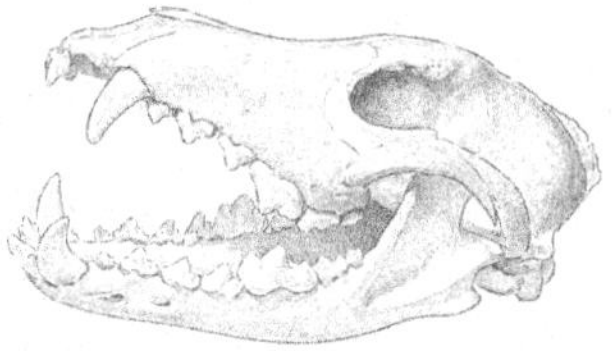

13
RHAIM

I waited until I heard Lisane's door close across the hall, repeatedly clenching the hand she'd licked into and out of a fist. It was exquisite torture that she had no idea at all what she was doing to me. And she wanted me to hurt *her*, when here I stood, hard enough to fuck through stone for the second time in one night. She knew nothing of how she left me.

I forced myself to calm down and breathe and somehow not remember the way she'd looked, wrapped around my shaft and trying to take all of me. So eager, so hopeful, plus—for once in our acquaintance—so willing to take direction.

And?

The most painful piece—

So ready.

I couldn't miss how blown her pupils were when I looked into them, or the press of her hard nipples against the linen shirt she wore, and I could smell her wetness flowing.

Even though she'd gotten what she wanted from me, it hadn't entirely been an act, as the current cleanliness of my right hand attested. And I'd only barely been able to hold back my knot. If I'd come in her mouth I wouldn't have managed to, no question.

I wanted to fuck her so badly that the thought of doing so made my beast rise up. If I took her—*when I took her*—it was only a matter of time—*and fucking Sibyi.* I cursed the other mage in my mind, because he'd been right without even knowing why. The things I owed Lisane as a man were different than the ones I owed her as a mentor, and if I trusted her desires enough for us to continue, I needed to concentrate on the latter for her own well-being.

I paced, feeling trapped by the small room.

If we were to continue, I could die tomorrow in her training, and then where would she be? It had been one thing when I thought she would be able to go back to her old life—but entirely another, now that I realized she would rather die than return to chambers.

So before we continued, I needed to make accommodations for her future care. There was only one mage on the planet who I would trust with her, and he was half the world away. As loath as I was to leave Lisane currently, I had no other choice.

I gathered up the consciousness of every nearby living creature that was not human to me. I felt a wave of them respond —birds sleeping in the eves outside, beetles burrowing in horse dung, a snake that was so cold it was only half-alive. Each of them said the world was calm, in their own perceptive manners, and I willed for all of them to guard her with their lives.

Then I opened up a portal.

I exited onto a wooden pavilion in a small mountainside garden, in the middle of the pouring rain, and suddenly in my heart, it was eight-hundred-some-odd years ago.

I could remember Malex the Icebringer, my master, a man as cold as his gift and twice as cruel, dragging me through a portal to land on this same pavilion, in rain much as this, the two of us waiting until Filigro arrived, so he could shove me at the other mage's feet.

I fell to my knees, having learned long before that complete obedience was the only way to avoid beatings, but I looked up at the new mage with sheer spite, waiting for him to pass his judgement. Filigro—now the Historian, but then the Nose—was the oldest of our kind, and he'd spent millennia scenting out liars in courts and wars on the wind before settling down here to accrue his books and devote himself to scholarship.

He'd bent over to breathe me in, all those years ago, then given Malex a despondent shake of his head, and I knew what that meant.

That my magic was nothing, and nothing would become of me.

I *knew* he was wrong.

I swore to myself then that I'd kill him for lying.

Malex, however, merely grunted, his suspicions about me confirmed. He took me back to his home in the ice, where I lived in a small room, waiting for a spring that would never come, and committed myself to studying twice as hard, driving myself like a boat before a storm, up until the day of my Ascension.

And after I had managed it, and knowing that my powers were far greater than some withered old mage had deemed them, I'd come back here to make good on my promise...only to find Filigro gardening with his partner, Parvel, nearby. He didn't seem surprised to see me, either—in those days, he could still see—in fact, he was thrilled to welcome me back, as if I were returning after a long absence, and not with murder in my heart.

He explained he'd lied to Malex to save me from the man's fits of jealous rage and pointed out that his lies had saved me not only beatings, but time, seeing as I'd pushed myself so hard. Then he invited me to tea and asked which books from his vast library would I be interested in reading.

I didn't trust him, but I was momentarily disarmed, and by my third mug, I was convinced enough to settle in one of the nearby caves that other scholars did when visiting for books. I spent a cheerful decade under his wing, reading whatever books I liked from his vast collection, experiencing the joy of studying magery for its own sake, rather than for a dread goal.

As I had never known my father—and even if I had, by now he'd be long dead—Filigro was the closest thing I had to one.

The door on the mountainside opened, revealing a familiar wizened man inside, with long white hair, a long white beard, and white-blind eyes, all wrapped up in warm robes. He breathed in deeply, and his face lit up. "Little beast!" he cried out.

I strode up the broken stone path to his door in the rain. “Old man,” I said. “I need your help.”

Filigro began waving me in as he stepped aside. “Drelleth’s princess—I heard—come in.”

I shook myself dry in the entryway to his cavern. Filigro’s personal rooms began just inside the door, in a large open space, which had his sleeping chamber combined with both his kitchen and his study. His famous library lived in the darkness of the vaulted caves beyond a locked gate.

“Tea?” he asked, after casting a light for my sake—I knew he was fully used to moving in the dark.

“Please.” I sat down on a bench carved into the far cave wall behind his table, pulling out my pipe. Nothing had changed here in the intervening centuries since I’d met him, except for the age that’d settled on his shoulders and the depth of the wear in the stone beneath my ass.

“Do you only visit when you’re in trouble, Rhaim?” he asked, opening up canisters of the herbal teas he made from the flowers outside by hand.

“And sometimes on holidays,” I protested, lighting up my pipe and breathing in deep. “For someone who doesn’t leave his home, you get gossip quickly.”

"The more delicious it is, the faster it gets served," he said, and once the fire was bright beneath the kettle, turned to me again. "So the stories are true?"

"Depends on what you've been told, I assume." I didn't like the idea of my own kind talking about me, but I had been the one to call a convocation and announce my business.

"Eh," he said, waving his head back and forth. "Rampant speculation mostly. Jaegar offered you his daughter for your aide, I know that much, but as to her fate since then—either you keep her chained to the wall and make her service you as you desire, or you've murdered her in a fit of beastly rage, and have carved up her body to eat to hide the evidence, right down to her very marrow."

I was glad he couldn't see the expression on my face. *Though I had certainly tasted Lisane...*"I'm as popular as always then, I see," I said, huffing out a cloud of smoke.

"You know how it is, Rhaim. Live long enough as a mage, and people start to forget that you're a person—you become an avatar of your magic, instead, even to your own kind." He returned with mugs of tea for both of us and sat across from me. "So tell me why you're here already. I'm dying to know."

"For an apparent immortal, that's saying something," I said, then went back to heavy smoking until my will was fortified.

"I need to ask you for a favor. I need you to say yes—and I need for you to then keep it a secret."

Filigro's hoary eyebrows rocked up over his glassy eyes. "Me? Who knows every mage on the continent? You are swearing *me* to secrecy?"

"Yes—is it a torture?"

He shook his head quickly. "On the contrary, little beast. I feel very pleased that knowing how active I am in the lives of others, you would still grant me your trust."

"Consider first that I have no one else to turn to," I muttered darkly.

He laughed. "Tell me. I will help you to whatever extent I am able, and I am prepared to carry your secret to my grave, should I ever manage to have one." He set his mug down, to breathe me in deeply, and I wondered just what his odd but powerful magic was telling him of my predicament.

I took a heavy draw on my pipe, and drummed my fingers on his table, bracing myself. "Should something happen to me —I need you to take the girl in."

Filigro instantly made a face and began to chuckle. "Rhaim," he said, stroking his beard with indulgence. "Even given another thousand years of life, I never would've guessed you'd feel softly towards anyone."

"I am not capable of love; I think we both know that," I said it easily, because I believed it to be true. My beast—the strongest distillation of my essence—didn't *love* Lisane. *He* wanted to own her. Punish her. Rut her. *He* wanted to take what he wanted from her, and give nothing back, until she was entirely consumed, and in that manner, perhaps, the rumors about me were right. "But I do care for her. She is mine—and I am doomed to die soon. So swear to me now that when that happens you will keep her safe. She cannot go back to her father, nor her former life."

Filigro's head tilted. "Has it occurred to you that you might continue living, if you bent your pride and gave her back?"

I snorted. "Of course. But I cannot." I took another heavy pull on my pipe, sending the embers in its bowl to the color of Lisane's eyes, then I realized how impossibly rude I was being. "Fuck, Filigro," I said, beginning to try and wave my smoke away from him. "It's been so long, I've forgotten—"

"It is no matter, little beast," he said, with a sorrowful head shake. "I smelled your death on you when you walked in. Of course after that, I would let you smoke indoors."

I put out my pipe regardless. "Would you have told me I was doomed, had I not mentioned it?"

"I make a practice of only telling people what they're capable of hearing," he said, giving me a bittersweet smile.

"Then tell me yes. It is the only word from you I can accept."

"Rhaim," he said, beneath his breath, his shoulders sinking.

"And I'm teaching her magic, too," I added, because I needed to confess—and, because, if Lisane did come into his possession, they would be the first words out of her mouth to him.

That brought him back to life. "Little beast!" he said, sharply. "How could you?"

"Stories about flames aside, I know full well the reasons we do not teach women, Filigro—so that old men cannot kidnap little girls under false pretenses. But she was *given* to me. I did not take her."

"Pah," he said, getting up to start agilely pacing around his sparse belongings. "I should call a convocation on you right now—"

"And what will they do—kill me?" I asked with a harsh laugh. "She wanted a life outside women's chambers, and I am trying to give her one. Do not tell me that out of all the other books in your library, I alone have committed this sin."

"Of course not—it's just that most of the others who tried were fools." He combed both his hands through his beard at once, and I knew from experience he was going to try to talk sense into me. "That pavilion outside, Rhaim—how long has it been there?"

"At least my entire life."

"And do you think it is still made of the same beams, from when you were young?"

"I doubt it."

"And yet it is still the same structure, is it not? So consider this, little beast—your heart beats, yes, but why must it beat for her? Why can it not beat for another? Perhaps if it did—it would get to survive."

I reared back at that. "And what would Parval say if he heard you say those words?"

"He would remember the name of the man I loved before him. And his ghost would remember the name of the man I loved after. And—above all else—he would not wish for me to be condemned." Filigro narrowed his blind eyes at me. "It is natural to consider teaching magic to the ones you love or think you do not, in your case. No one wants to see their lover age and die, I know that more than most. But do not flout our rules, Rhaim, and waste your remaining time. I scent her virginity on you—at least go and bed her, and reduce your life by one folly."

"But that is the thing, old man. My time is not wasted. She has skill—and I can teach her." I played with my pipe in my hands, aching to light it, and fearful that Lisane was being stolen, back where it was night. "So promise me—" I pressed him.

"I will not."

I only barely stopped myself from growling at him. "Is this how you die, old man? Do I kill you to keep my secret?"

Filigro fell into the seat across from me again and reached out, catching both my hands in his briefly, to shake. "Rhaim—you do not hear me. This is worse than cannibalism! Eating her—you're a beast—perhaps that could be forgiven. But teaching her magic? That comes from your man! A man who makes choices, knowingly!"

"Tell me why I shouldn't, then," I challenged him.

"Because! If you succeed—she will be barren!"

"She does not care."

"She won't survive her Ascension—"

"Some mages don't; it's true." I shrugged, forgetting he couldn't see. "But I suspect she would be willing to take that risk."

"And the fire?" he pressed.

"Have you ever seen a woman catch fire from learning magic?" I made a scoffing sound. "She has not combusted yet, old man, so I don't think she will. And if I am not afraid, and she is not afraid—there must have been others, surely, before us, equally fearless."

"Rhaim," Filigro said, pleading with me to have sense. "Of course, you would not be the first, and of course, other mages have managed it!"

I felt a wild spark of hope catch flame. "Then tell me of them."

"I will not. Because none of their situations, in any way, compare with yours."

"Bah!" I growled. "Filigro—"

"No, you will listen to me!" he shouted. "How many men have true magical talent to begin with? Divide that by twenty, thirty, and then divide that by women given the opportunity to learn from mages willing to teach them."

"It is a small number—so?"

"So—if she were a peasant girl, maybe, *maybe* you could hide her light. If you abducted her, took her halfway across the continent, started a new life, trained her—and if she survived, let's not forget that! If you turned your back on your own powers, never magicked a beast again, crashed your castle, and left your precious library behind, it is possible that all would think you dead, and you and she could live a semblance of a normal life, forever or until fate took you—as some extraordinarily few others have." He stood, and began pacing again. "But with this girl, Rhaim? It is impossible. You're trying to train the princess of the king the rest of the Seven have decided to bow down to, during our current crisis. Jaegar will never truly let her go, not while she is still of use to him."

I inhaled to rebut him or defend myself, but he quickly raised a hand.

"I dislike the man as much as you do, but think, too, how you would be condemning her!" he said with a stomp, and then pointed at me. "I remember your youth, when you poured through men and women like water, and as far as familial attachments go, you might as well have been an orphan, except for me. But like her, I had a family—a people. A country." He punctuated his words by thumping his own chest, before gesturing wildly around himself. "Where are they now? Lost to time, alive only in my memory! So—knowing how lonely this life can be, would truly you wish it on another? Especially when you are on the cusp of death and will abandon her yourself?" His loud words echoed around us in the cavern, and when they stopped, he spoke again at softer volume. "Be rational, Rhaim, for once."

Every word he had said was true, I felt it, and yet I could not give him what he wanted. "Promise me."

He pounded a fist on his stone table. "There is not such fertile soil for vows here! Just give her back!"

And for his sake, and the sake of our long friendship, I tried to imagine it, but I could not.

Because at the merest thought of relinquishing Lisane, I remembered seeing her through my beast's eyes, standing at the edge of the torn hole in my castle, with her dress fluttering behind her in the wind and only the sky beyond, as she readied to jump.

Some creatures would rather die than be tamed—even by me.

"I am not just teaching her for my sake, Filigro," I said softly, willing him to understand. "I am teaching her for hers. She will never live without windows again, as long as I draw breath."

The much older mage shook his head with sorrow. "Then you condemn her—and yourself."

"Me? Yes. Her—I do not know. But you're the only one I can trust with her, and none of our kind will act against you. So swear it to me—on Parvel's grave, and any others that you've loved."

"You doomed fool," Filigro said, but I watched him sway, and knew that I had won. "I will not train her further, Rhaim. She will only get as far as she gets with you."

"Just don't let them put her into chambers again," I said, moving to stand. I needed to go outside and portal back. I needed to know that she was safe. "She has made her choice. And I have made mine."

I began walking for the door, but he called after me. "How much have you taught her?"

"Not much. She has raw power, mostly focused in times of need. I can feel it in her, just underneath the surface. I would show you the scar she's given me, if you had eyes to see it."

"And her magic's cost?" he pressed.

I held my pipe in one hand, and looked to the palm of the other, the same hand I'd spanked her with, choked her with, and the same hand she'd licked clean. "It is profound. Yet she is willing to pay."

He huffed another breath in. My own nose wrinkled, and I wondered if he scented Lisane the same as my beast did, almonds and honey combined, but I knew better than to ask.

"Wait here. I will give you books to take back," he said and portaled away. Every second he was gone, I grew impatient, my beast rising to the surface in my fear that even now, someone was stealing her. Then he returned, with a large stack of journals to hand over. I gave them a cursory glance, but he shook his head. "They're not for you—they're for her. She deserves to know what she is getting into. Perhaps she has more sense than you."

"All things are possible," I said, as I took the books from him.

Filigro swatted a hand up to draw my head down, to kiss my forehead as though I were a child, and when I stood, I paused. "In all the rumors that you've heard—does anyone ever suppose a version of the story where I'm not hurting her?"

He put a heavy hand on my shoulder. "She is the Princess of Tears, Rhaim—of course, everyone assumes you make her cry."

14

LISANE

The next morning I woke to the strangest sight I had ever seen. I lit the lamp at the foot of my bedside, and it illuminated a startling line of mice looking at me, with their beady black eyes, and then behind them a row of beetles of some sort, and a snake, and a handful of crickets, all of them just...watching me?

"Shoo!" I said, my word breaking their spell. All of them scurried for the crevices of the room, and I squeaked without meaning to, worried that some might crawl into bed with me in their flight.

I gave a careful look before I set my foot down, not wanting to squash anything, then I stood up and shook out my boots before putting them on. When I opened my door I found it was covered in webbing, too. I touched the broken strands. *Was this what being a consort was?* Instead of surreptitious surveillance, I was to know I was watched at all times?

I steeled myself to weather whatever mood Rhaim was in and knocked at his door. When he didn't answer, I found it unlocked. He hadn't even left his book behind for me to read.

I wasn't sure how to feel, walking downstairs into the rest of the inn. Pella spotted me immediately though, bringing my breakfast and two shiny coins. "He said to give you these," she said, then grinned. "You should tell him you're worth more."

I made myself laugh for her sake, as I took them, trying to seem normal—I didn't even know what denomination they were, but I knew what I was to spend them on, and just what it would mean.

It was what I wanted, yes—to feel magic flowing through my veins, and for me to do great things with it. But I was haunted by its cost: how I would earn it, and who I would earn it from.

I made myself eat, and then stepped outside. Rhaim was at the well again, surrounded by innumerable beasts and people, with industrious children hawking bread and ale to those in line. I pulled my cloak tightly around myself, but it was too late—he looked across the backs of forty ewes and saw me. His expression did not change though, and after a steady moment, he looked away, going back to his work nearby.

The coins in my hands felt heavy.

It was time for me to do my work, too.

Jelena caught me walking up the street as I walked down it, and there was no dodging her. She gleefully pulled me aside. "So?" she asked in a leading fashion. "How do my brother's pants fit you?" She feigned innocence, but only for a second, then cackled. "What was it like? Did it hurt? Did you have a good time?"

I could feel myself turning brighter than an apple. "I did what I needed to do."

"'I did what I needed to do,'" she echoed in disbelief. "Are you really just going to leave me there, Lirane? After all the help I gave you?"

I did feel bad, but I had to go from here on out alone. "I am. It worked, though. Thank you. But now I need to run some errands, to help restock the castle."

"Can I help?"

I quickly shook my head. "No, sorry. The castle is a private place. You know why."

She pouted. "Fine, all right. Just as long as there's not anyone else you're telling here instead of me."

"There's not. I promise. No one else here would even begin to believe me."

"Well, if you decide you can share," she said, giving me a wicked look. "You know where to find me."

"I do," I told her, then scooted around her to continue on my way.

The local shopkeepers had been all too happy to help, especially the rope one, who wanted to guess what exciting animal it was that Rhaim would be using the rope for. He got as far as guessing gryphons before I made my escape. For the cane, I found a woodworker and grabbed the least embarrassing length he had smoothed, some piece that had been meant for decoration, a long rod the width of my thumb. Armed with the rope over one shoulder and the cane beneath my arm, I returned to where Rhaim was, in the middle of a mass of swirling livestock, and knew he'd see me.

When he did, he stood.

I could hear the farmers grumbling, but their beasts parted in a wave to let Rhaim pass—not toward me, but through the throng, toward the edge of town. I paralleled him along store and home fronts, almost jogging to keep up with him, until he was past the last of the animals, finally turning toward me.

His mood was no mood at all, and he kept his expression completely still as he addressed me. "And have you done as instructed, little moth?" he asked, even though he could clearly see I had, as I was carrying both items. I frowned a little.

"Yes, sir."

He paused, as though hoping I would reconsider, but then said "Very well" before putting his hand out. I gave both the cane and rope over, and two horses trotted up, the massive piebald work-horse again for him, and a leaner bay gelding for me, attentive and prancing. "I already paid their owners for their time, this morning," he said, moving over to the bay's side, turning his hands into a stirrup for me, so I could ride as men did now that I was wearing pants. I stroked a hand along the horse's side, feeling the heat of the sun reflecting off it. In another, simpler life, I would've gotten to do nothing but this all day, just feeling the fur of a willing beast beneath me.

"How beautiful," I whispered.

"Indeed," Rhaim said, drawing my attention back to his presence, where I caught him looking at me as he shook his hands again for my boot.

He mounted his own horse, and we rode for quite some time in silence. I passed the time watching our surroundings and petting my horse's neck. The bay danced beneath my seat a little, like he wanted to run, but wasn't sure where to go—rather like I felt. I wound my fingers into his mane, turned to Rhaim, and caught him watching me again.

"Whatever it is, just say it," I told him. He stopped my horse with his magic and wheeled his own in front of it, then pulled out the cane I had brought, holding it like an unsheathed sword.

"Is this what you think of me, moth?"

I looked between him and it. "I...don't know?" I guessed, unwilling to be wrong, and thus unable to be right.

His frown deepened, and he tilted his head, imploring me to think. "Would you really want me to hit you with this?"

I truly looked at the cane I had brought him—stiff and thick—and swallowed. "I don't think so."

"I happen to *know* so, and moth, that just won't do." He shook his head in a weary fashion, tucking the cane back beneath his arm again. "I asked you to do one task, calmly and clearly, a task that you at the time were eager to take on—to buy the heaviest cane you thought you could take—and instead you've brought me this thing which I wouldn't even use on my workhorse here, much less a fragile girl." He considered me, and I could tell he found me lacking. "Either you were seeking to curry favor by offering yourself over for a beating, which means you don't understand the point of this instruction, or I cannot trust you to be honest with yourself about your limits, which makes me worried to teach you."

I flushed with anger at myself, that I had already made a misstep. "It was neither!" I protested quickly. "I got embarrassed at the wood shop—I—"

He held up his hand for me to stop talking, so I did, trying my best to be obedient now. "Why do you think high-born women are trapped in chambers?"

I blinked at him changing course. "I've always been told," I began slowly, trying to hedge my bets, "that it was to prevent things like this from happening." I gestured between us, a little frantic. "Even though you won't tell me how I came to be in your possession—I did not ask to be here."

"And yet you won't go back?" he asked, his voice entirely flat, his entire demeanor still dismissive of me.

"Never," I answered instantly.

His eyes narrowed. "Perhaps they are trapped in chambers because they find magic embarrassing," he said.

I stiffened and then panicked. The town was far behind us but his castle wasn't on the horizon yet, and I wasn't sure where we were headed. "Rhaim—you promised—"

"*Bah*," he said, powerfully. "You are mine. I am not returning you. But I have more questions, let me ask them." I swallowed, nodded, and pressed my heels lightly against my horse's sides, wishing I could urge it forward against his will. "Why do you think women do not learn great magic, moth? Aside from the fear of flames?"

"I don't know, sir." It seemed best to go with utter honesty, now.

"It is because men like me cannot be trusted with the likes of you—much less tempt you to be barren."

His words took the knife of dread he'd already stabbed into me and twisted it. "If you tell me that having children is magic enough, so help me, I will find something to throw at you, Rhaim."

Finally, his lips pulled up. "Isn't it, though?"

I didn't know if it was a tease or a taunt.

"You think I can't find the same enjoyment in studying as you?" I demanded.

"But what if you find yourself unfulfilled?" he casually asked and shrugged lightly. "Do you really want to feel empty for eight hundred years?"

"I don't know—why don't you tell me how that feels?"

His eyes flashed at me, and he snorted before continuing. "I only ask because there are things we need to discuss before your training continues."

"Then let us discuss them, and stop trying to scare me." My horse danced sideways beneath me as I mastered myself. "Sir," I added, belatedly, and he gave me a curt nod.

"Fine. It is possible, moth, that we train you and nothing ever happens. That your skills, whatever they are now, are the limit of what you possess."

I did not want that to be the case, but I understood why he might feel the need to warn me. "All right."

"And it is possible that if your training continues, you will die."

I made a face at him but otherwise tried to exhibit patience.

"You remember all the spelled parts in the journals that you've been unable to read?" he asked, and I nodded. Almost all of the journals he possessed had strange gaps in them, sometimes just a paragraph, others, entire pages, and once half a book, that no matter how hard I tried, I couldn't get my mind to decipher. "It is because I've been hiding the facts of our Ascension ceremonies from you, when we become able to portal and gain our mage-marks. Not every mage survives the transition. As the pain of Ascension itself is indescribable, I cannot imagine dying during it is any better."

I swallowed and nodded. "I understand," I told him.

"Good," he said, and made a grave sound. "This is why I need you to imagine going back, right now, for your sake, Lisane." His gaze was steady on mine. "If you find the idea tolerable for even in a moment in your mind, you should do so."

Panic rose again in my throat like a winged thing. "You tell me I am yours, and then you tell me I should go?"

"I am full of contradictions," he said calmly. "And I can't have you training out of a fear I'll send you back—which is what this cane says to me." He flicked the cane's end with a finger.

"It was a mistake. A lesson, which I've now learned." I considered getting off of my horse and running to him to grab his leg and plead. “Have I backed down from any of your challenges yet, sir?”

“No,” he said. Rhaim took a deep, deep inhale, and released a heavy sigh. “I care for you, Lisane. And I don’t want to see you waste your life solely because you think you must.”

It was what part of me wanted to hear, some acknowledgment that I wasn’t just entertainment for him. But then I remembered who we were to each other, and how we’d been the night before, and my hands tightened in my horse’s mane. “Did you care for me before last night? Or did my lips suck caring into you?” He said nothing in return to that, merely continued to stare me down, until I wilted. “Sir,” I added, quietly.

Many more uncomfortable moments passed before he spoke next. “And that is exactly why I must ask you these things, moth. I need you to know that you may stay with me of your own accord and not train—that you don’t have to suffer my hand or risk your life to experience your freedom.”

I stared down at the bay’s neck, abashed. “And actually be your consort?” I asked quietly.

“Only if you desired it,” he said. “Although consorts are generally more agreeable.”

I dared to look up at him again. “Had many, have you?” I asked, both frightened and curious of the answer.

He gave me an imperious look. “No. I could count the people whose presence I find tolerable on the fingers of one hand.” He urged our horses forward again, letting mine pull alongside his. “I just don’t want you to look back on your life with regrets. These could be the end of your fully human days.”

I looked around at the broad expanse of blue sky overhead, at the grasses lining the sides of the road, feeling a light breeze lift my hair, as we were surrounded by bird and insect-song, all of which were things I hadn’t even had time to get used to, yet.

If this was being fully human...what had I been before?

“Do you regret your change, sir?”

“Not in the least,” he answered, then glanced in my direction. “But I have always been like this.”

I knew what his “this” was: difficult, cunning, possessed of frightening moods. While I wasn’t exactly the same as him, I was just as sure of who I was.

“Me as well, sir,” I told him. “I just never had a chance to *be* it before now, was all.”

I watched him as we rode, and heard him take a massive intake of breath that had just a hint of a growl to it, then release it with a nod. “I believe you,” he said, turning toward me fully. "So renounce your humanity and your world, and come join me in mine."

He said it casually, like the phrase held no special meaning, but I knew it marked the beginning of a mage's real training, from having read it in my books—and I knew exactly what to say back to him. "My world is no more, and my humanity is no longer. I am yours to train."

His lips lifted up into a subtle smile, then clucked his tongue, and I felt my horse perk up. "All right, little moth. Let us go faster, so we may begin. Hold on."

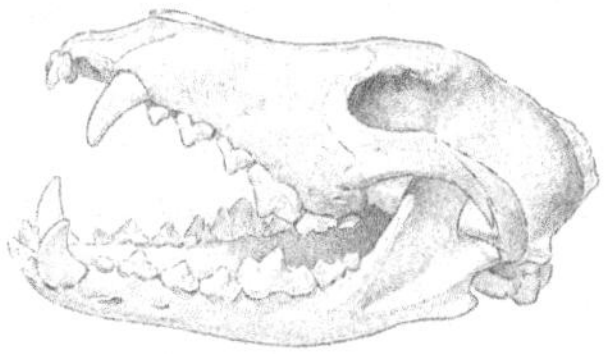

15
RHAIM

Within seconds, Lisane was shrieking with delight.

Her horse was ten feet away from mine, and not going anywhere near as quickly as it could've—it was much more nimble than the workhorse I rode—but it was still faster than she'd ever gone before. Her fingers were laced tightly into the bay's mane, and she was leaning forward and down to one side, my old cloak fluttering behind her in the wind, laughing from her heart.

I was glad she'd found boys' clothes to wear from somewhere, seeing as it made her slightly safer on her horse—and I was glad she hadn't stained her cheeks or lips again. If she did it for her own sake, that was one thing, but I didn't want her to do it for mine; I would take her as she came to me.

And it was just as well the cane had forced the issue of our conversation. I didn't need that particular implement to do anything to her, my castle was full of options—but I did need to know that she would listen.

The farmers I'd left behind in town, on the other hand...I kept telling them I was leaving soon, but it didn't seem like they believed me. Word of my arrival had spread, and now there were people who'd come from quite far away in line, and on my way to the horses, I could tell some of them were angry. That was the real reason why I didn't stay in towns for very long—eventually, people would start taking you for granted, thinking that you owed them...but if you performed strong enough magery to make them fear you, that also led to trouble.

It was just easier to stay away from people entirely, rather than face their continual disappointment—with the exception of my moth, whose future disappointment in me I courted every day.

She would learn how I came to be in possession of her eventually—and the truth was, I should tell her before somebody else did. But I hadn't figured out a gentle way to disappoint her yet. And as much as I longed to crush her memories of her father, her brother, Castillion, and everyone she'd ever known with their betrayal of her innocent trust, I knew the fact that I *had* taken her would dye me just as darkly.

Perhaps I would die before then.

It would be easier on me.

I made an irritated sound at my gloomy thoughts until Lisane's whoop distracted me—she'd spotted the castle on the horizon. I waited until we were halfway there to settle our mounts down to a walk, and the look she gave me then was of pure joy.

"Rhaim, I liked that," she said, breathing almost as hard as her gelding was. She had a natural seat on the bay, I could feel it in the way the horse responded to her, and it made me wish she were riding parts of me, instead. "Can we do it again?"

I couldn't help but smile at her. "Not without lathering them. I don't want to injure them—plus, they're not ours."

She twisted to pucker her lips and narrow her eyes at me. "But you do want to injure me," she said.

I could hardly deny it, as we both knew it was true. "You belong to me," I said, because I knew from taming wild things that half the battle was getting the beast used to the collar. "There's a difference."

My little moth pretended to be affronted at that. "I don't actually belong to you, Rhaim. I just want to learn," she said, moving her seat and making her horse prance sideways.

I managed to keep a smirk off my face. "Then would you go off with another mage, if he offered to train you?"

She tossed her hair back and fluttered her eyes at me. "If he brought me horses? Yes," she said.

I laughed, and then sobered at the thought. "It is time to talk of other things regarding your training, then, Lisane. I know you do know other mages—but if something were to happen to me, you can only trust one named Filigro." I watched to see if his name sparked anything in her eyes, but it did not—just a panicked frown as she rose up, her knees squeezing the bay tightly.

"What? Why?"

"Have I ever struck you as unprepared?" I calmly asked, willing the same for her.

"No," she said, slowly rocking back.

"Then assume I am merely covering any eventualities. Filigro is a good man. He will take care of you."

She gave me a stricken look. "I do not want to be taken care of."

"I will never clip your wings, moth, but others would. And until you are possessed of your own powers—and the ability to portal, after your Ascension—"

"All you can do is hand my reins to another," she finished for me. "Would he continue my training? Did you tell him how I work?" Her hands let go of her horse's mane and she held herself, pinching at her own skin by way of illustration.

"I did not...and he likely will not. But his library surpasses mine, and he is kind, I swear it," I said in earnest, but she couldn't hear it. She was breathing roughly, and her amber eyes were distant and unfocused like they were once more looking out at a blue sea. I nudged my horse closer to hers until our knees touched, and that contact gathered her attention. "Little moth, don't panic. He once helped train me —he gave me books for you to borrow."

"I thought you said your master beat you." I could hear the concern in her tone.

"He did until he couldn't anymore," I said and shrugged. "But Filigro didn't make me a mage—he made me the man I am today." She didn't respond, merely kept watching where our knees jostled, lost in thought. "Though you should assume that all my many current flaws are my own, for his sake," I teased.

She finally looked up, still haunted. "Rhaim, you cannot leave me."

Did she truly want me, or just the freedom that I brought her? My body didn't care; my heart was like a mouth inside my chest that swallowed her words whole. "I have no intention of ever leaving you, Lisane."

"Promise me," she demanded, willful despite the tears hovering in her eyes. "Sir. Please."

I made both our horses stop. "You are like a storm trapped in a girl." I reached over to her then, running my fingers through her hair and tightening them, so she couldn't look away from me, so I could tell her as much truth as I could stand. "How many battleships of men do you think I would kill for you?" Her eyes went wide and she shook her head, inhaling to speak, but I shushed her. "The answer is all of them, moth," I told her. "But I am still mortal, and you are still untrained, and whatever truce I have with your father I cannot guarantee. And so, you must also trust Filigro, as I do. Even if not for your sake—you must promise it for mine." She slowly nodded, though she still looked pained. I let go of her hair and set her loose.

"I should've never written him," she whispered.

I shook my head, wishing she wouldn't blame herself over my half-truths. "What's done is done, moth. We cannot change the past, nor predict the future. Best to only stay in the now. From here on out, I want total obedience, Lisane—and also total honesty."

Her eyes squinted and her expression was wary, but she still nodded, and I began to let our horses move forward.

"I need to know when your attention is flagging. When you're in a bad mood for no reason. When you're hungry or when you're tired. If you have a question, I want you to ask it. Pretend I like nothing so much as the sound of your voice."

My little moth snorted softly. "You might wind up regretting that."

"I fully intend to," I told her. "I want to push you as far as you can go, as quickly as we can, but," I said, pulling the cane out from underneath my arm again, "a broken moth won't do. So I must rely on you to know your limits and be honest with yourself, so that you can, in turn, be honest with me. Can I trust you?"

She gave me a look that was somehow both unsure, and yet completely determined—I felt it was her natural state. "Yes," she said, definitively, and then added, "sir," as an afterthought.

"Ahh. The sweet sir of obedience at last," I mocked her.

She laughed at that, regaining some of herself, and I watched her lips part as she took a breath, weighing what she would say next. "Why do you tolerate me not saying 'sir' all the time, sir, if it is truly important to you?"

"Because you keep remembering that you've forgotten them—which means even when they aren't on your lips, you feel their echoes in your heart." She groaned lightly beside me, and I pressed. "And what mood are you in now, little moth?" I was annoyingly solicitous, on purpose.

Her eyes flashed. "Since you want honesty—irritated."

"Because I am right," I said, feeling smug.

She pouted. "And now? I almost hate you. Sir."

"It is no matter," I said, giving her a wicked grin. "It will be the first of many times in my instruction," I said in an ominous tone and watched her brow furrow, even as her pupils widened and her nostrils flared. "So prepare yourself," I warned her, and urged our horses into canters.

16

LISANE

I didn't know a word for how I was feeling.

Everything had wrung me out.

Between the embarrassment of buying the wrong cane this morning, up through the repercussions it had had, and knowing what was coming—it was too much to think about, and so I didn't want to think at all. I just leaned over the bay's neck again, urging it to go faster still.

But I believed Rhaim when he said he wasn't going to let me go. Something had changed, after we'd made our promises to each other—and I already knew his words had meant more to me than anything spoken under an arch of unicorn horn ever would.

And I believed him when he said he'd kill more battleships of soldiers for me, as stomach churning as the thought was.

I wished I could go back in time and wrest my foolish letter away from my foolish hands and thus stop myself from ever revealing who had trapped me. I had been operating under my old beliefs, that whatever my father wanted was the right thing to do.

But my father would've never granted me this moment, and my mother would've been aghast, were she still alive.

No, I would've never gotten even so much as a solo ride. In pants, no less.

With newly pierced ears.

I gave my horse's neck a secret smile. My life was mine, and I was racing toward a future I was desperate to attain.

We arrived at the castle, its walls covered in scaffolding, the open tear in its side slightly reduced. Rhaim stopped our mounts a bit away from the laborers, who mostly appeared to be taking a break, except for a few who were roped to the highest floor.

I swung a leg over and dropped down, petting my horse's side. "Can we ride them back?"

"How else would they get home?" Rhaim said while smiling.

And now I had another ride to look forward to—no matter what else today brought.

"I'm glad—" I started, just about to wax on about the majesty of horses, as I heard a commotion behind us. I turned and saw a stout-looking man blustering through the rest of their ranks.

"Get on your knees!" he shouted, and his men, who'd watched us come in in silence, did as they were told, hurriedly setting bowls and cups aside.

Rhaim's face went dark with disapproval. "This had better not be for me, Ajeil."

"No—it's for her," he said, pointing.

At me.

I started wildly shaking my head, and whispered, "Rhaim," while stepping forward to hide behind him. Doing so let my cloak part, so the man could see what I was wearing, and then he looked confused.

"I'm sorry—I see you're a trader—I assumed you were highborn," the man said.

"She is not. *She* is *mine*," Rhaim growled and gave the surrounding men a dangerous glare. "So whatever you were doing prior, continue." He turned to walk beneath the scaffolding and I followed him closely.

"How did he know?" I whispered, waiting for him to undo the magics he'd put upon his door.

"He was just guessing, without context," Rhaim muttered, letting us into the castle's protected antechamber. "It is one of the many reasons I claimed you as my consort in town—far easier to start a rumor than to suppress one."

He opened the door, and I looked back the way the man had gone. "And you're certain he doesn't know me?"

"Very. We are far away from your home, by design. And he will not think of you again tomorrow."

"But—"

"Do not let it scare you, moth." The look he gave me then was complicated. "As much as I hate to divest you of your innocence—most people outside of castles do not think of high-born girls much. Seeing one of you is like seeing two rainbows at once, or a shooting star. Noteworthy at the time, but by no means life-changing." He set the lock to the door behind us and then began opening the castle's true entrance inside. "They look forward to the celebrations when you're born, and the holidays they get when you get married. That is all."

And some small part of me that was still attached to my former life was horrified. In the castle, my tutors and maids always made me feel important. Plus, I could bend my father

—the king's!—ear. I spoke before I could stop myself. "Am I truly so inconsequential?" Rhaim made a pained face that told the truth. "But I have never even seen a rainbow or a falling star!" I complained. "I've only read about them in books!"

"Well, no one has ever given me a holiday—so let's go tell Finx hello," he said, taking the loop of rope off of his shoulder, and opening the door to let me through.

Rhaim's spider-cat was waiting inside the next door for the both of us. "Lisane!" he shouted, flinging himself at me. "I missed you!"

"I missed you, too!" I said, catching him. It was so strange to think that I'd once thought his many legs frightening, as he now used most of them to cling to me.

"What have you been doing?" he asked. "And are you okay?"

"I've been with Rhaim, and I'm fine," I said, stroking the bristly fur of his body as he purred wildly. "But thank you for asking, as we both know how irresponsible he can be," I went on, because Rhaim was in earshot. "He forgot to bring me books to read. Even though he came back and got some for himself."

"How rude!" Finx agreed.

Rhaim rapped my ill-bought cane against the stone wall below us for our attention. "We didn't come home so that you two could gang up on me. Finx—go back to keeping an eye on the workers. Lisane and I have business to attend to, but we will dine with you tonight."

Finx compressed himself against me, then sprang off onto a wall. "I don't like them," he complained to Rhaim. "And they don't like me."

"I don't like them either," Rhaim said, waving him on with one hand. "But they're almost done."

Finx bobbed, patted the air in my direction with his two front legs, and then zipped up to the ceiling for the library.

"As for you, moth—go bathe and put on a dress again." Rhaim said, brushing by me. "When you're done with that, walk up a flight of stairs, and you will find a new door."

Then he portaled away, and I was alone.

I was ashamed that my first thought was of disobeying.

It was beautiful and sunny out, and I'd seen the scaffolding on the castle coming in and the workers tied to it for their protection like they, too, were spiders. None of it reached the castle's roof with his tub, outside...but I couldn't very well have pledged my loyalty to honesty and learning, then ignore Rhaim's first request.

I got to my bathroom and undressed, taking off my cloak and the rest of my "boys" clothes, stepping into my unscenic tub to scrub myself clean and try to prepare. It was a strange thing to know that I was *going* to get hurt, and I couldn't say that I was looking forward to it.

But physical pain had an ending.

Whereas never getting to *ride* a horse again?

That was unendurable.

So I got out, dried myself off, and then reached for the dress Finx had made for me, which he'd lightly stuck to my bathroom wall.

It was still made of pretty spider-silk, but the front was made of overlapping panels, some of which were missing across my hips and ribcage, and it had a high slit up the side. I could already hear Jelena laughing. *Did your man pick that out for you?* Indeed.

I put it on with a frown and stomped into the hall barefoot, walking up a floor.

There was an open door there, just as Rhaim said there'd be, and the room beyond smelled like animals when I walked inside. I wasn't surprised to see saddles and bridles hanging off one wall, or bales of hay, for all that we were in a windowless room inside a castle.

And Rhaim was already in a corner, his back to me, getting something ready. His hair was wet, the same as mine, so I knew he'd also bathed.

"What is this place, sir?" I asked him, announcing my arrival.

"It used to be a tack room and a stable," he said, returning his attention to me as he walked back—this room was the same length as the library, though not as high ceilinged. He'd created a stack of hay bales, and placed some sheets across them, and I was thrilled to realize that he was setting me up to do target practice—like my powers were a kind of archery.

"I used to keep all sorts of creatures, especially when I was studying them."

"And now you'll be studying me?" I asked.

A brief smile flashed across his face. "Seems like."

There was a table to my left that held all sorts of implements, some of which I recognized—whips, with tails short and long—and others, like cruel hooks and metal rollers with spikes that I did not understand. And on the ground at the end of the table was a rather large cage. He caught me staring at it, and laughed. "That's for magical creatures, not moths. Don't worry."

I swallowed. "Thank you. I think."

"You're welcome," he said, and cocked one eyebrow as he took me in, leaning against the table full of devices. I had my arms wrapped around my chest, somewhat afraid that his strange dress would fall down if I moved wrong, and partially trying to hide myself from him. "You don't like it?" he asked, and I thought he might be trying to hide a smirk.

"Dresses usually have more fabric, sir."

"Ah, well, you'll have to believe that I have a reason."

"Oh, I believe that you do, sir," I told him. "I just don't think I like it very much."

He chuckled at that, and stood, walking to be behind me. “May I touch you?”

Considering why we were here, it was such an odd thing for him to be asking. “Yes, sir.”

“Good. Are you empty of magic now?”

I searched inside myself. “I think so?”

He made a rumbling sound at that. “Then I shall have to fill you up.”

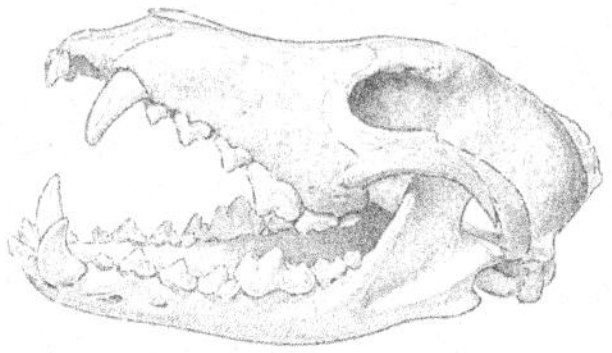

17

RHAIM

My moth thought her only motivating factor was pain, but I wasn't so sure, seeing as each time I'd hurt her had had elements of shame and humiliation as well. Once I'd returned from Filigro's the prior night and checked in on her, I'd come here to prepare for today, devising ways to quickly test her abilities, until I'd returned to the town at dawn to wait her out.

"Stay facing that way," I told her, and went to the table with the tools on it, to pull a chair out, set it behind her, and sit down, pulling out my pipe to light.

"Sir?" she asked, as the smoke rose up.

"Remember your promises to me, little moth," I said, clenching the pipe's stem between my teeth, as I crossed my legs.

"Yes...sir," she said with hesitance.

"Lift your skirt up, and get down on just your knees."

Her fingers fumbled with the edge of the sheer silk dress Finx had made her, picking it up slowly, but still doing as she was told.

"A little higher, moth." I clucked. "And spread yourself a little wider."

She waddled her knees out, almost showing herself to me. "Sir—" she began to question, as I slid my boot between her thighs.

She froze, as I pressed the top of my boot against her and shifted it, imagining her folds dragging against the leather like it was a tongue.

"Am I hurting you now?" I asked her.

She hadn't moved, but she was breathing in short, sharp bursts. "No," then added, "Nothing but my pride."

"A useless thing, where magic is concerned," I said, stroking against her carefully. I'd polished these boots the moment I'd gotten this idea, and I had to say I was pleased—I would be thinking of this when I fucked my hand tonight. I gently rubbed her once again with the top of my boot. "Ride me."

"Sir," she said, her tone a protest and an acknowledgment of her position all at once, but then she did as she was told. I felt her settle back and slowly began to rock. Her hips stroked back and forth, and I was treated to the view of her perfect, heart-shaped ass wriggling as she ground herself against me.

She made a sound, and I didn't know if it was good or bad, but that wasn't the point—*this was*—I reached forward and grabbed up all her wet hair, pulling her head back, and her body off balance. "Faster," I said, subtly kicking.

"Rhaim," she spat like my name was a curse, but then I felt it, an easing of the friction between her flesh and my leather. I scented her sweet release as she slid against me easily, and I knew my poor little moth's juices were slicking the top of my boot, even if she didn't want them to.

I willed my hard-on to subside and somehow dropped her hair and pulled my boot away. She caught her breath, then looked back at me over her shoulder, like I had betrayed her, though I wasn't sure how—*by starting, or by stopping?*—with a flushed face and her full lips softly parted.

I blew out a cloud of smoke in her direction. "Did you feel shame?"

Her hands fisted into the hem of her skirt, and she nodded, even though her nipples were hard.

"Did you feel humiliated?" I asked her.

"Yes," she hissed.

I uncrossed my legs and put my elbows on my knees. The top of my right boot was glistening with her wetness and I longed to make her lick it clean. "Did you feel magic?"

She blinked back tears. "No."

I made a satisfied sound. "Then that experiment is over."

18

LISANE

I gawked at Rhaim, feeling like a disheveled mess, as he went on. "How do you feel?" he asked.

It was hard to look at him—but it was also hard to *not* look at him because if I looked down I would see how he'd left me, and how I'd left his boot.

His. Boot.

I gathered my will to be honest as I'd sworn I would. "I want to throw myself at your feet, but also claw out your eyes."

Rhaim gave a dark chuckle. "As I warned you. You will wind up hating me quite a bit. Don't let it get in the way of your learning." He stood and walked off, heading back to the table, and I scrambled to stand, to try to regain some decorum.

I expected him to return with a whip, but instead, he brought another chair and set it across from his, indicating that I should sit down. I did so, the slit on the dress exposing my thigh up to my hip, and he and I both knew what had happened between my legs.

The difference between us was that it only bothered me. I wished I had even one-tenth the control over myself that he exhibited.

After he sat and puffed, he offered the pipe over. "Would you like to smoke?" I shook my head. "So be it," he said, shrugging lightly. "Tell me of all the times you have ever managed magic, moth. Don't leave anything out."

I tried to regain my focus: I inhaled, exhaled, purposefully imitating the calmness he radiated, before going on. "My mother knew how to cup light. It was the most useful skill to have, living in our chambers. But she wasn't the first one to teach me."

"No?" he asked.

"No. It was a mage, when I was five or six. We were outside —I've forgotten why—he told me to try to reach for the sun, that if I tried hard enough, I could catch it and put it in my pocket for later." I concentrated harder on the memory, until it felt more real to me than my recent upheaval on the room's floor. "I tried all morning, all afternoon, stretching my little hands up to the sky, trying to grab hold of the light and failing. I wanted to catch it so badly I was crying when we had to go back to our chambers again. But the mage promised me if I thought hard about it every day, if I looked into my hands and remembered what the sun had looked like when I'd put it there, if I practiced and I hoped, eventually I'd manage it. And a month later...I did."

"Which mage?"

I looked at the ground and said, "Castillion." Rhaim growled, and I felt guilty.

Shouldn't I still be mad at him for killing Castillion? At least a little?

Just how faithless was I?

Then again, I'd followed Castillion around, begging for him to teach me more for the next thirteen years, and he'd been unwilling, whereas Rhaim...

"When else?" he asked.

I closed my eyes, and I continued. I told him of every time that I ever even thought magic might've worked for me, making it easier for me to see while doing needlepoint in dim lighting, and healing the blisters that I gained from too tightly holding a stitching frame—both of which seemed wildly underwhelming now that I knew what I was capable of—up until the moment when I'd wound up in his dungeon.

"Surely you read about everything afterwards though, sir."

Rhaim crooked his fingers in my direction. "I did not read so many pages before I felt the need to yell at you, moth, so please continue."

I licked my lips. "Fine. After you chased me and I managed to cut you, and then after you spanked me, when I broke the table...I thought I realized what the commonality was. So I experimented on myself."

"And then with me," he finished.

"When I had you whip me, yes."

"And the outcome?"

"I saw my family." The look he gave me then was strange, so I pressed on quickly. "When you left for your studies the next day, I tried to do—anything, really. I tried, and tried, and failed. But I was in front of my mirror, and when I'd almost given up, I saw an image of my father arguing with Helkin, and my name upon his lips."

He pulled his pipe out of his mouth and played the stem of it across his teeth. "Which is why you wanted to send the letter."

"Which I now vastly regret," I said, bowing my head.

He shrugged that away, brow furrowed in contemplation. "Moth, that's quite powerful."

"It is?" I asked, looking up. "Can you do that?"

He shook his head. "I can see through an animal's eyes...but not at such a great distance as you managed. We were very far away from your father at that time. What was its price?"

"A headache so bad I thought I would die."

"But you didn't," he said, the corners of his lips lifting.

I gave him an excited half smile in return. "I did not."

"What was next?"

"The next time—you were mad at me." I encircled my throat with my own hand. "You choking me let me light a candle's flame—and the price of that felt like burning."

"And with Vethys?"

"He was rough with me when he grabbed me." This elicited another growl from Rhaim. "But him doing that—it let me push him back, and rocked his ship. The price of that was broken ribs."

"He is dead now," Rhaim said.

"I think I knew—but I never said thank you."

Rhaim nodded, and then stood up to pace. "At any time, did you feel your powers come up upon you? Like they were something you could direct?"

"Not really, no."

He grunted at that. "Stand up and turn around again, moth—if you're feeling up to it, we should continue."

I stood up by way of answering, and he took my shoulders from behind, lining me up with the distant hay bales, then standing very close behind. "Whatever powers you use—warn me before you use them, if you can, and aim them that way. But also try not to set anything on fire, or hurt any more of my castle. Or me, for that matter."

I whipped my head to look back at him—and my eyes caught sight of both his demeanor and the scar that I had given him. He wasn't making fun of me; he was deadly serious. "I understand, sir."

"Good. May I touch you again?"

I braced myself, readying for anything. "Yes."

And at that, he wrapped his arms around me, engulfing me easily. He was taller than I was, broader times two, and his arms were thick with muscles. I'd been so worried he was going to use another tool on me, I'd forgotten about the man himself. I swallowed, trying not to be afraid.

"Will you warn me, sir?" I whispered.

"This time, absolutely," he swore, and his hands came for my chest.

They slid in between the dress's missing panels, skin on skin, each of them holding my left breast, one from above it, one from below it. No one had ever touched me there before, and I fought not to flinch against him in surprise. I could feel the strength in his fingers, and the roughness of his palm. "I've done nothing but think about how to train you, little moth, since you left my room last night," he told me. "How best that I could cause you pain."

I didn't know what to say to that; I just watched the space where he held my breast, cupping it like it was an injured bird, which was fitting with how fast my heart was beating nearby.

"There are many lines of thoughts to torture," he went on. "And more reasons to do it to another than you might think." His thumbs stroked me calmly. "Are you waiting for me to hurt you, Lisane?" He kneaded my breast a little, pulling it up with both his hands, just on the verge of pinching.

"Yes," I whispered.

"Does the anticipation make it worse, or better?" He moved his lower hand so that his thumb and forefinger could lightly squeeze my nipple, teasing it into a blunt peak. That made me sway against him—and then he took it, and he tugged up until I rose up on my toes to follow with a gasp. He slowly brought it down, I rocked back, and he released me.

"Push the top of your dress down," he commanded, and I did as I was told, quickly unlacing my arms from the straps. To think I'd been worried about how much skin I was showing prior, and here I was now, eagerly presenting it.

Rhaim took a look down at me over my shoulder, and made a sound of satisfaction. "Such soft skin, moth," he said. "So easy for me to mark." He cupped my breast again in one hand, and drew a fingernail from his other hand over it, sending a ripple of sensation through me as it left a trail of red behind.

"This is the only place I'm going to hurt you," he said, then did so, squeezing my breast roughly from below, lifting it up again, and then forward, before using it to press me to him, with a dark snarl in my ear. "Just this one pretty, perfect breast." He reached his other hand around to pluck at my nipple and then ran the pads of one finger over it in rough circles—before licking them, and returning to do the same.

"Rhaim," I whispered, arching back into him, trapped between his arm and chest. The spit he'd circled me with was cooling and I wriggled helplessly, making small noises as I ached.

"How do you feel, little moth?" he asked, pinching my nipple again and pulling up, harder this time, farther too—and then when he dropped my breast his strong lower hand grabbed me in a rough promise. "Tell me how you feel, moth," he said again, a demand now, not a question.

My jaw dropped. What I felt—how I felt—was not something I wanted to put into words. That I should tell him that I wished he'd let me ride his boot to completion—or that I wanted him to push me down and enter me on his stable's wooden floor—it was unthinkable—I couldn't—

Then he slapped my breast and I gasped his name. "Rhaim!" I said, jumping.

"Glad to see you still have words in you," he said—and then slapped me again, a little bit harder, before licking his fingers and tugging at my nipple again. "I asked you a question, moth. Answer it," he said, and once more raised his hand.

"Confused!" I confessed quickly, hoping to avoid his wrath. "And hungry," because it was the truth.

But I wasn't the only one. I could feel the thick, hot length of him, trapped inside his leathers behind me. And I made the mistake of reaching back for it—he shook me, then smacked my breast again, making me whimper.

"That is not the point," he growled.

I made a sound I wasn't proud of. "Then what is?"

"Breathe," he warned me, and then slapped my breast—from the top down, and then the bottom up, one side and then the other. I cried out as his free arm snaked around me to hold me still as I pushed against it, and he hit me again and again. I dove my face into his neck, to try to stop from crying.

If he wanted honesty, he would get it, "Rhaim, you're hurting me," I said, trying to squirm away.

He paused, and I was still pressed against him, so I could feel how roughly he was breathing. "Did you want me to stop? Or did you need me to stop?" he asked, and I realized the subtle difference between the two questions.

My poor breast was marked red, and I could feel it beginning to swell—but I could also feel the beginnings of my power stirring. Now that I'd been a conduit, the sensation of it filling was easier to place.

"Moth?" he pressed, his lips beside my ear.

"I wanted you to stop," I confessed. "But," I continued, unsteady as I caught my breath, twisting my head to face him, "I—I need more." His arm cinched around me, pulled tighter in response. "Sir," I gasped lightly, licking my lips.

Rhaim made a sound then that slithered inside my ear, sank down my center, and coiled in my core. "Then loop your hands about my neck, little moth, and do not hide yourself from me."

I gave myself over, standing on tiptoe to wind my arms above myself, running my fingers behind the nape of Rhaim's neck, through his hair.

He kept hold of me with one arm, then held the other out so I could see it change, his hand shifting, the hair on the back of it thickening as his fingers lengthened and five black claws came out.

"Rhaim—" I panicked, squirming, and he held me tighter still.

"Shh. It is still me," he said into my ear, and then brought his clawed hand for my breast, palming it entirely, so that each of his claws made little divots in my flesh. He drew his hand out slowly, letting his claws dance across my already-reddened skin, making me hiss, and then when he got to my nipple, he pinched it in between two of them. I opened my mouth in a silent scream, as twin drops of blood appeared, one to each side, bright red against his claws' black.

Everything in my body said that I should run away—except for the place inside my hips that throbbed.

"What if I pierced your nipple like your friends pierced your ears?" he asked, in a low, growling tone. "Then I should only need to tug on it to empower you."

Clarity flowed over me like a living thing—a shining moment, breaking through the fog of pain.

If Rhaim had *truly* asked...I would have let him.

I would let him do anything to me.

The realization was as frightening as it was freeing. It took me somewhere transcendent, even as it made me sway.

He carefully let go of my nipple and loosened his hold on me. "Moth—breathe." He was right—I felt dizzy—and my knees were weak—"*Breathe,*" he commanded, with more force, spinning me around. He stroked the back of his still-clawed hand across my cheek, and I felt the fur there, tickling against me. It made me want to laugh but I wasn't in myself anymore. It was like I was seeing everything we were doing from a distance. "You are all right. You are with me. And we are through."

I blinked, reminded of who I was and where I belonged, feeling my spirit and my body conjoin again. "Wait—no—" I protested weakly.

"Either there is power in you now, moth, or we will wait until tomorrow." His tone was stern.

"Just—give me a moment. Please." I took the liberty of grabbing hold of his leathers, to keep myself upright, swallowing, my body feeling like a lead weight to me, now that I was in it—and no part of me was heavier than my tortured breast.

Rhaim swiped his thumb across my nipple—it felt like it was on fire and made me cry out. "Poor, sore moth," he crooned, bringing his thumb to his lips to lick my blood off before he picked me up to carry.

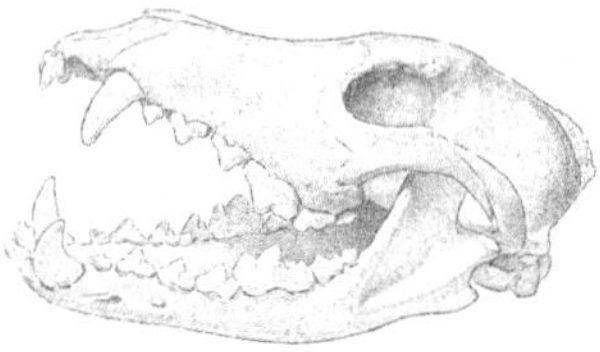

19
RHAIM

Lisane fell asleep in my arms before I reached her bedroom door.

I could only barely recall what learning my magic felt like, the things that it had cost my body as it changed it, giving me my second form and my knot, and I had no idea what hers would do to her.

But I did remember being tired—and Malex shouting at me for being "lazy"—which was something I would never do to her.

I laid her down in her bed, unmade like she'd left it, with her dress still half down, her breasts exposed to the air, her hair tangled from rubbing against my leathers while it was wet—she looked like the victim of a ravishing. And I had been very cruel to her...but cruel because she let me. Hopefully, she would remember that when she woke up.

I sat down on her chair, to watch her sleep and read one of the books that Filigro had given her. I'd briefly skimmed them the prior night and most of them read like manifestos of obsession, instead of journals like they ought. It made me wonder if Filigro was trying to warn my moth about me.

Whereas my own journal had been full of blank pages, almost ever since I'd met her. Anytime I thought to write in it, I balked.

And hers?

Had been left open on her desk. To a drawing of a moth inside a birdcage. I frowned, and closed it for her, tracing one finger across a fractured emerald on its cover. I must have broken it on the stone of the roof when I'd dropped it in anger.

Finx scurried in across the ceiling, and took in Lisane with all eight of his eyes. "What did you do to her?" He accosted me, dropping and flipping adroitly to land on his feet in her bed. He pointed at her with one foreleg, and then the other at me. "You hurt her!"

"I did—" I said casually, beginning to explain, but he leapt to be on the side of her bed closer to me, throwing up his front legs and showing me his fangs, chittering.

"Finx!" I chastised him, standing quickly. "Stop this at once!"

"Lisane!" he said, kicking her with one of his hind legs, hoping to rouse her—while protecting her from me. "Lisane!" he urged.

I patted the air between us. "She is sleeping off her magic, Finx."

He let his forelegs drop with reluctance, spinning this way and that, to eye her and then me. "But her dress—"

"She took it off willingly."

"And her skin?"

"She wanted me to do that." I couldn't lie to him and say she'd be whole when she woke up, but I could tell him the truth. "Her magic pains her—it is her price."

He made a disgruntled sound, and started pulling out webbing to cover her back up, pacing it out quickly from his spinnerets. I stepped up to the bed to watch him work.

"You have been my creature for centuries," I complained.

"So?" he asked, sounding sullen, turning to cast his webs upon her.

"So—did you just choose her over me?"

Finx paused, but only for a moment. “And what if I did?” he said, bobbing up and down defensively, before tapping at her with a disconsolate hind leg, illustrating her fragility. “She doesn’t have a shell like you and me, Rhaim. She needs protecting.”

I sank to sit on my heels in front of him, bringing us level. “I know.” I looked between the two of them. “And I know I’ve failed you both, before. I’m sorry.”

“Thank you,” he said, winding his forelegs around each other with anxiety. “I’m sorry too—”

“No. Don’t apologize.” I had no idea if Finx would survive my death, being my magical creation. But if he would… “This is how I want you to be. I will never do her harm, Finx, but others would. She needs you more than I do. And if you have to ever choose between us—choose her. Promise me.”

He tilted his body wildly, so all eight of his slitted eyes could see me in turns. “Are you certain?”

“I mean it more than anything.”

“All right,” he said, with an affirmative bob. He wheeled back to her and petted her forearm with a pedipalp. “She cried for me, when she thought I’d died.”

“She is a sensitive sort,” I said, standing up again.

I could hardly tell my spider-cat that Lisane had cried for me, too, many times now, for entirely different reasons.

20

LISANE

I woke up in my bed with a headache...and stuck to the sheets behind me by a thin skein of webbing.

I sat up, breaking through it, instantly reaching for my breast. It felt like someone had stabbed me. I cleaned more of the webbing away to see it for myself—just as hot, swollen, and sore as I feared. And my mouth was dry, and I needed to pee...

I got up and pulled the remnants of my dress back on. The last thing I remembered was Rhaim, and his claws on me, and then me thinking I'd let him do...

Anything.

Anything.

The memory still resonated inside me, and all of what it could mean came spilling forth. His hand in my hair, his cock in my mouth—*and other places*—him hurting me—and me...just at his mercy.

Like I had been earlier.

Total abasement.

I could feel my powers now, like a tightly wound snake—but I could also taste the bile of panic on my tongue.

I went to the bathroom first, then made my way upstairs, into the dining room, where I found Rhaim sitting at the far end of his table like he always did, reading while facing the stair door.

My place setting had been moved though, to be right next to his.

Where he could easily touch me, for better or worse.

He snapped his book shut at the sight of me and stood up. "Moth—are you hungry?"

I put a hand to my stomach. I was...but everything else was all tangled up inside me too.

He moved around the table, to take my arm. "Come. Sit down. Drink. I'll get you food." He helped me to the chair, and disappeared for a time, until he brought back a bowl, some kind of porridge with cream on top. He set it in front of me and then sat down beside me, apparently to watch me eat. "Have you had water yet?"

I nodded. "In the bathroom."

"You should drink more," he said, pouring a glass from a carafe and then proffering it to me. I took it and set it aside.

"Why didn't you put me in your tub to heal?" I asked, and when he didn't answer quickly enough, "Because of the workers?" I guessed.

His eyes on mine were dark. "No. Because some people like to see their marks later, and I didn't know how you'd be."

It took a long moment for me to parse his words. I put a hand to my chest, not in pain now, but in horror. "You've done this to other people before?"

"Yes."

"So you just go around hurting people? All the time?"

His brow rose in bemusement. "Not hardly."

"Just a select few, then?" I asked, arch.

Rhaim rocked back and waved his hand in the air between us. "Get it out, moth. Say what you're really thinking, rather than jabbing at me to provoke a response."

My hands clenched into fists on the table. He wouldn't even let me be in charge of my own anger. "It's not fair," I said, knowing as I said it I sounded childish. And it wasn't like any of my life had *been* fair, up until this point. But I still had a sense of balance inside of me. Rhaim had totally upended it, and I didn't know what was going to take its place. "And even though I understand that—and why it's like that—it still makes me mad." I glanced up at him and caught him trying not to laugh. "You don't know what this is like!"

His eyes narrowed, and I watched him purse his lips. "I don't, do I?"

"No," I spat. "How could you?"

He stood abruptly at that, his chair spinning out from behind him, wood scraping against wood. "Come with me," he demanded and went for the stairs without waiting to see if I'd follow.

I wanted to dig my heels in. I wanted to fight. I didn't want to be made complicit in my own destruction; I wanted him to come back here and grab me and pull me after him, kicking and screaming, for him to finally break me—like I knew he longed to—so I wouldn't have a choice.

And I also knew that he would never, ever do that.

If I stopped moving forward of my own accord, he wouldn't push me—he'd pull back.

"Moth!" he shouted for me, from somewhere below.

"Coming!" I shouted back weakly, getting up, hugging myself as I descended the stairs.

When I got to the stable, the door was open, and Rhaim was already there.

With his shirt off.

And he was kicking off a boot.

"Sir?" I asked, all of my pity for myself forgotten.

"It is a poor man who asks others to endure what he hasn't himself," he said, fingers reaching for his leather's laces.

I gasped and turned around before he could show himself to me. "Sir," I said. I heard him moving around, behind me, before giving a short grunt.

"There. Turn around, moth."

I did so slowly, uncertain what I was going to see—and utterly surprised by what I found. Rhaim was kneeling, facing away from me, and somehow he'd tied his hands behind his back.

And . . . his back . . . .

The scars of his that I had seen, the ones on his arms and across his chest, were random, of differing depths and thicknesses, so that I could tell he'd earned them all at different times, presumably from beasts.

But his back bore the signs of being beaten. Scars that were similar in ages, the same color and thickness, the kind that when he'd gotten them, must've made him sleep on his stomach for a month.

"Rhaim," I whispered, more disarmed by the visible marks of violence on him than by his nakedness.

"Do not look at me like that," he said, without turning around.

"Like how?"

"However you are now. With sorrow or softness. Stop. I am teaching you, and nothing more."

I frowned deeply at him, even though he couldn't see. "Then why are your arms tied? And why are you kneeling?"

"Because I want you to take up something from the table and hit me."

My jaw dropped. "I will not."

"You will. Otherwise, we will not continue."

"Rhaim—"

"Not all pain is pain, moth. You forget I could feel you yesterday. Hear you. Smell you. And while I may have hurt one small portion of your anatomy, the rest of you...it was not mad at me at all. You're not upset with me because I hurt you. You're upset with yourself because you liked it."

I inhaled to protest...and then realized he was right.

How fair was it that he didn't even need a whip to flay me?

"So go get something from the table, and try to hurt me back."

I stood behind him, breathing hard. And then I wheeled to do as I'd been told, swiping up the first thing on the table that I could reach. It was some kind of whip made of many heavy leather tassels. I raised it up, watched his arms flex and release, as his head bowed—and I brought it down.

The leather strips thudded on his back, adding brief red marks to his many white scars before his magical health disappeared them, and Rhaim chuckled.

"Moth, you will have to hit harder than that if you want my attention."

I froze, as angry as I was unsure. "You also collared me," I said with spite. Surely he would not—

"Go cut a rein and leash me."

My nostrils flared. I went to the table, picked up a knife I hadn't known was there, and ruined a piece of tack, returning to him. I walked around in front of him on purpose, because I wanted him to see—and he gave me a delighted smirk.

"You're incorrigible," I complained, tucking the whip beneath my arm so I could loop the rein around his neck.

"You are the first woman I'll have ever let hit me."

I stepped back. "Which means...you've done this with other men before?"

"Mages live a long time, moth," he said and shrugged. "Oftentimes, it's lonely."

I tried to give him the courtesy he'd so often given me, of only looking him in the eye, but from this vantage point it was hard...because I did want to see. The brand of his mage-mark was clearly visible on his chest, and his cock hung down between his legs, wrapped in its sheath, the tip of its head poking out, with the thick metal ring looped through it, the whole heavy affair resting atop his balls.

"You may look," he said, and I flushed, caught, determined not to.

"Did you do this with your master?" I asked, angling my eyes up at the ceiling.

"The same man who beat me?" I heard him scoff. "No. Whippings and beatings are different, moth. The latter does not engender affection. If I had let my master tie me up at any point in time, he likely would've left me outside in an ice storm."

I frowned. "I know what you got out of your bargain with him—but why did he teach you if he hated you so?"

"There is an expectation that you will do some training in your life. Other mages will look at you unkindly if you don't."

"So you were...an obligation?"

"I was. I also chopped a lot of wood for him. And summoned animals for him to slaughter."

"Your only value to him was as a source of food?"

"Yes. But stop stalling," he said, with humor in his voice. "Were you going to hit me or not?" I stomped around to be behind him again, his "leash" tight in my hand. "Really put your arm into it, moth. Try to hurt me, just the once."

I pulled my arm back again—and swung it at him, full force. I heard the tassels hit his back like the patter of rain, him make a satisfied hiss, and a moment later, all the marks upon his back were gone. "You heal so quickly."

"You sound disappointed," he said, rocking back to stand up. The knots behind him came loose, and he freed both his arms. "You will heal quickly too, given time. Do you think most people recover from broken ribs as quickly as you did?"

Him being naked in front of me, standing, was even more distracting than him on his knees. He seemed oblivious to that fact as he undid the rein from around his neck.

"I thought it was the bath," I said.

"Some, but not all. Magic makes us more resilient, so that we may suffer longer," he said, and offered the rein out to me.

I took it...wondering if he would use it on me next.

And wishing that he might.

"Should we see if we can shake any of the magic we put in you yesterday out again?" he asked, sweeping up his leathers from the stable's floor to pull them on.

"Yes, sir," I told him. "Please."

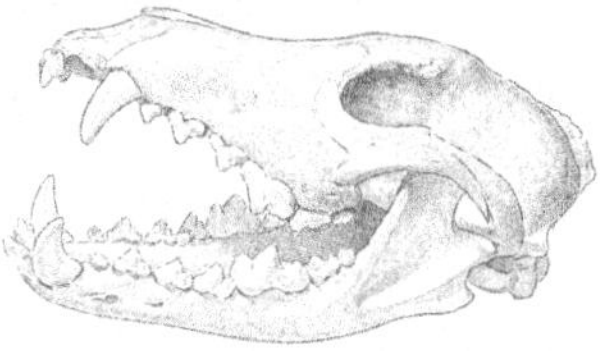

21

RHAIM

I had no idea how Lisane's powers would exhibit themselves, and thus wasn't entirely sure where—*if anywhere!*—would be safe for me. So I set her up in front of the targets, brought over a chair, and pulled out my pipe.

"What am I supposed to do?" she asked, holding herself in front of me.

"Pretend there's still a whip in your hand," I said. "And aim it."

She nodded, and I watched her jaw clench, her brow furrow, and then she turned around. If magic was an art based on stubbornness alone, my moth would rule the continent.

She threw her arm at the targets...and nothing.

“Again,” I prompted. She did so, to no effect.

I watched her try, perhaps a hundred different times, in many, many ways, until she growled. “I wish they would explode!”

I pulled my pipe out of my mouth. “Maybe don’t wish for that, inside my already-broken castle.”

She rewarded me with a tiny smile. “I don’t understand though, sir,” she said, clutching a hand to her belly. “I can feel it inside. I know it’s there. This time, it’s not a mystery.”

“How long did it take you to cup light again?” I asked her.

“I hate when you’re right. It’s irritating,” she muttered.

I laughed. “Time and patience, moth.” She gave me a look at that that said what we both knew: time we might not have...and patience she did not possess.

I stood and walked up to the bales, pulling out a strand of hay before then returning. “Not all of my powers manifested at once, little moth. When I began, I could only call creatures to my side. Pretend it is the smoke. Begin.” I held the straw out to her. She took it, and I sat down again.

CHAPTER 21

Hours later, I called an end to things, practically pushing Lisane out of the room while she complained. "But I'm not done yet."

"Because you can't finish what you haven't started," I said, chiding her gently. "I let you sleep in this morning. But it's dinner time now, and neither of us has eaten all day. You're not a mage yet; you're still quite mortal."

"Stop reminding me," she said, looking at the entirely intact hay bales across the room with venom. "Sir," she griped.

"Well, your mortality means I'll even let you go up to my bath to heal."

Her eyes lit up at that. She inhaled, then paused. "I do want to go outside again...but I feel much better now, already."

"Small magics, moth. Good. Go bathe, and then return to eat."

When I was done cooking for us, I returned to the dining room, to find her in an unsullied dress, with her hair in a braid, and reading a book—one of the ones Filigro had lent to her.

I brought dinner out, pleased to see she'd already emptied the water carafe. "This is not such a good book, Rhaim."

"Why not?"

She tilted the journal so I could see she'd almost skipped to the last page. "She dies."

I made a growling sound, cursing Filigro, as I put our food on our plates. "I'm afraid he means to scare you off."

She closed the book and set it down. "Did you tell him that was impossible?"

"I defended your honor in every way," I said, coming to sit beside her.

She gave me a courteous nod. "Thank you."

We ate in silence, and my moth ate everything I'd put in front of her, plus another serving. "Will the townspeople get upset that you weren't at the well today?"

"Most likely, yes," I said dourly and shrugged.

"And don't you need to go study some?" she asked.

I hadn't thought to lie about why I wasn't leaving—and now that I wasn't serving her father, I had no reason to go. "Worry about your own business, not mine."

She swiped her finger across the remnants of the gravy on her place and licked it, while contemplating the door just past me. "I wish we could go into the library, Rhaim."

"Why can't we?"

She glanced back at me, surprised. “Because they’re fixing it—”

“Only on the outside portion,” I said and stood. “Let’s go see.” I cupped a tiny light in my hand and stood to lead the way.

There was a stiff wind outside tonight, making the protective webbing Finx had spread billow inwards like a sail. Finx was inside the room, monitoring this, tacking down edges as they lifted. He spotted me—and ran over to Lisane.

Good spider.

Lisane cupped light of her own and brought it up, casting a subtle glow across her face.

If the webbing were gone, we would’ve been able to see the moon outside—but it didn’t matter.

I could see my moon, right here.

I held a finger to my lips for silence, and we snuck across the room to the web, to listen in.

Ajeil’s men had hung enough lanterns on his side of the webbing so that there was no way they could see ours, and we could hear the workers outside, hammering and talking amongst themselves.

"It's unnatural, is what it is," one of the men complained. "Spiders shouldn't get that big."

Finx jumped out from behind Lisane's skirt and pointed an accusatory foreleg at the men behind the curtain.

"And you never know. Is it just the one? Or is there a whole—I don't know, what do you call a shit-ton of spiders, Jole?—could be more than one inside—"

Another man grumped. "Spider this, spider that, if you don't like the money, Samen, don't take the job."

"I'm just saying—all this webbing has to come from somewhere!"

"What's unnatural is having to listen to you complain about this every night."

"And you've never even seen it yet!" someone else chimed in.

"Well, we're almost done now, ain't we?" Samen said, sounding almost disappointed.

The temptation to raise up an army of the spiders that I very well knew were available, out there in the field where they camped, was large. But somehow I managed.

Lisane, on the other hand, crouched down and whispered something to Finx.

My spider-cat ran up halfway again to the curtain and threw his front legs up—while Lisane got low behind him and made her light *shine*. Finx's shadow rose up, ten times as big as he was, and I heard the laborers shout in surprise on the other side.

I snapped my fingers, and they both cut it out immediately, but Lisane was covering her mouth with her hand to hide her laughter and Finx was running around in triumphant circles.

"You could've killed someone!" I hissed at her, more amused than mad.

"They're all tied up—I saw it when we were riding in—"

"I give you magic, and this is how you use it?"

She winced. "I wasn't thinking."

I caught her protecting one hand with the other and frowned. "Was the cost worth it to you?"

She looked between the wall of webbing, outside of which the laborers were still resettling, a preening Finx, and what I suspected was a very sore hand. "Yes?" she guessed. "Sir," she said more firmly, trying to earn my favor.

"Bah. Grab a book and get to bed."

"Yes, sir," she said, still trying not to laugh.

I picked up a random book and swatted her direction in a harmless threat. She giggled and ran off, and I made my way back into my own bedroom to read.

I spent just as much time looking into the fireplace as I did looking at the words that night, trying to dissect my rational thoughts from my intrusive feelings. It would be easier if they were apart from me, like when I was learning the inner workings of the beasts I could control. Then I could just pick them away like so many extra bits of meat and bone until I'd carved them down to the level that made sense—a tendon pulling a claw here, a bone moving in a joint.

But right now everything inside of me was too inextricably entwined to pull apart.

I wanted her.

She was just two floors away from me here in my castle.

And some piece of her—naïve and inexperienced—wanted me.

The man who was doomed to die at her hand.

I could mostly ignore that fact, now that I was used to her presence, and my intermittent lust. But I wondered if not telling her about it was a bigger betrayal than not telling her about my arrangement with her father. If she did manage her Ascension—and when she found out what that meant—then she would know the truth.

That there hadn't been a moment, ever since we met, that I didn't see my death inside her eyes.

I could only hope that that shame of her learning that would be absolved by a second realization: *that I had loved her anyway.*

For as much as a creature such as I was capable of it.

I tossed the book I held into the fireplace, as there was nothing good in it and I needed to watch something that wasn't my heart burn. It went up in flames, and as the leather binding let out an acrid burst of smoke, I heard a soft knock at my door.

I stood and went to answer it, finding Lisane on the other side, naked except for a dress she had torn down the center, to wear like an open robe. Her shoulders were set, her lips were parted, and her eyes were bright.

"I believe as your consort, there are other things I am owed."

Whatever magics had channeled through me during my Ascension were nothing compared to the strength I was using right now. I took a great breath. "No."

"No?" Her tone was sharp, her countenance wounded. "You made it sound like it would be my choice. I am here. I have chosen."

"No," I repeated, and held up one hand, to silence further protest. "It would interfere with your learning."

Because it would destroy my ability to teach her.

If I started bedding Lisane now...I knew I would not stop until I knew her in every way it was possible to know a woman.

"You told me you didn't always want to hurt me," she said, sounding confused.

"I did. And that is true."

"I don't understand, then. I want to feel like that again—and I know you want me."

I was glad she wasn't looking down. "Of course I do. Any man who didn't would be a fool. But I am a mage, not just a man, and I have other responsibilities." A pretty flush rose over her and she grabbed the sides of the robe she wore, wrapping herself in it protectively. "Go to your own room now, Lisane, and do not come for me in mine again."

She stared me down for another moment, then spun, walking away, her chin haughty but her shoulders slumped, having no idea how close I was to claiming her in this hall.

I wanted to tell her to run, so my beast could chase her down after three steps, listening to her frightened screams as *he* took her to the ground. He would tear the silk she wore away with a stroke of his paw, and use the other to drag her hips up so he could enter her ferociously. He would not care that she was a virgin, nor would he be soft—*no*—he would take his fill of her, pounding her while she cried out—from fear, from pleasure; he wouldn't care. He would snarl in her ear, scenting the blood from her skinned knees, until he found his satisfaction, and he wouldn't warn her when he was about to blow. He would just come in her like she was meant to take him, shooting himself into her in thick, hot, bursts, his cum leaking out from her cunt until his knot sealed them, keeping her trapped below him, letting out low, rough grunts, still thrusting even though they were mated, just so he could feel how tight she was.

And then she turned the corner and somehow my sanity returned.

It wasn't until hours later, all that time spent pacing in front of my fireplace, considering whether opportunities lost should be regained, when I realized what she'd said.

22

LISANE

It was a good thing I was becoming familiar with humiliation.

I walked away from Rhaim's bedroom, wishing I could melt into the ground. It would be easier than facing him tomorrow morning—I had no idea what I'd been thinking...

Except that wasn't true.

What had happened was I'd gone back to my room, and hungered, and then apparently lost my mind. I wondered if magic did that to you too; if in addition to making you go through your personal reserves and strength, it also ate your common sense and pride.

I'd lain there in my bed, staring up at the ceiling, feeling the weight of the magic I now carried in me—that I didn't know how to access yet, like a burden I couldn't quite set down—paired with the same feeling that'd ridden me on prior nights, a tense and prickling need. An urgency in the place I wanted him to feel and fill, the kind that made me rub my thighs together and made me slick.

One of them, I couldn't do anything about.

The other…I hoped I could.

Up until Rhaim had rejected me.

And if he was smug about that for even one moment tomorrow, I would figure out a way to shoot my magic at him.

I was still staring at the ceiling, counting down the minutes to my shame, when he burst in, holding both my rope and cane. I sat up on my bed and kicked back, holding my sheet to myself—he yanked it aside without asking.

"Don't worry, I'm not going to use this on you," he said, dropping my cane to the bed, unspooling the rope from around his shoulders. "At least not like that."

"Sir?" I squeaked.

"Lie down," he commanded. "Face up."

I realized I'd curled up. I put a careful leg straight as he loomed bedside—he'd installed some sort of metal hooks on the cane, on either end—and he took the ankle I'd put down and laced it to one of these with the rope.

"Rhaim?" I asked, but he didn't answer; he just snapped, and pointed to my loose foot. I gingerly extended it, and he started tying it to the cane's other side, so that my legs were spread.

He took in my condition with something akin to satisfaction, and repeated himself. "Lie down." I squirmed down the bed so that I could, and then he put his hand out. "Your right hand. Give it to me."

I did—but he didn't take it. He only took my wrist and pulled it down, running a knot around from it to the cane between my ankles, so that my arm stretched over my chest and my hand was set between my legs.

He took a moment, more to inspect his knot work than me, then sat back down in my chair, before pulling his pipe out, and kicking up his heels on the edge of my bed.

"Sir?" I wondered.

"Touch yourself."

I blinked at him, my mouth gaping open like a fish's. "You're joking."

"Not in the least, moth." He gestured at me with the pipe. "Begin."

I stared at him for several breaths, waiting for him to laugh, but he didn't. "How is this—" I started, but he interrupted me.

"Do you not know how?" he asked. I felt myself turning a blazing shade of red, like my whole body was dipped in berry juice, and one of his eyebrows cocked up. "An intrepid mage like you, I would think you'd been practicing, ever since I licked your cunt."

This proved it. I would never truly be magical, because if I was, I would've incinerated myself—*or him!*—with my embarrassment.

"I consider myself responsible for all facets of your education, moth," he said, lighting his pipe and giving it a contemplative suck. "And this is another thing you must learn to please me."

"I cannot believe you, Rhaim—" I said, giving my ties a thrash.

"Do you need more lessons?" he asked, with maximal sarcasm. He stood and spit on the fingers of his right hand, before leaning over and placing them between my legs. I shivered at the sudden contact, gasping as he slipped over me, my nipples pulling tight. "Right here, moth," he said, rubbing in a circle. "Touch your clit here, where all things meet." His eyes began on mine, but then he glanced to where he touched me. I swallowed to see the hungry way he looked at me—and I wanted to squeeze my legs shut to keep him there, but couldn't, with my ankles tied as they were.

Then he pulled back abruptly and reclaimed his seat. "Finish yourself before I finish my reading."

"Is this another kind of torture, sir?" I whispered.

"You tell me," he said, wiping his hand off on his leathers before picking up a nearby book.

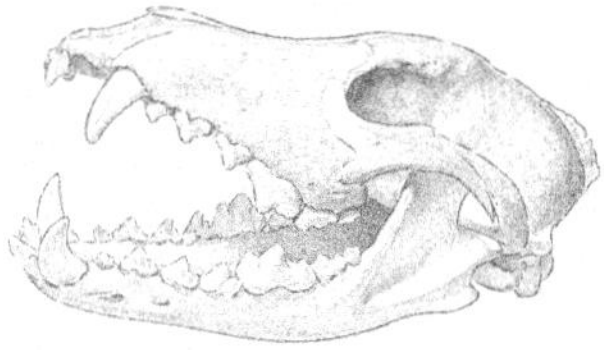

23
RHAIM

I sat back down, and found myself reading the journal of Agarwath the Invisible, who used his powers for thievery, mostly. And if I recalled correctly he could technically still be alive somewhere for all anyone knew, seeing as the price of using his magic was slowly becoming translucent. His journal ended rather abruptly—I remembered something about him having an eye on something that "wasn't his" and was the "mayor's prize possession," which could've been a daughter, a wife, or a cow—who knew?

But he was one of the olden ones who'd gotten Lisane into this mess. Mages who did as they pleased, taking and hardly ever giving back, ones who used their powers solely for personal gain.

It was when someone could not only portal in to steal your "possession," but could *portal in unseen*, that locking up your daughters like livestock started to seem like a good idea. That, combined with magery making women barren, and also possibly providing them with opportunities to escape, is what had directly led to my innocent little moth here, who was studiously *not* looking at me, as she tried *not* to touch herself.

"If you don't take this seriously, it will only get worse," I warned her.

She pouted at the ceiling. "This feels silly."

"Magic often is. Continue." I blew a cloud of smoke out in her direction. And when, after another handful of seconds, she didn't move—I made the shutters on her windows fly open.

Her room was beneath the scaffolding, looking out at the workers traipsing up and down the wooden planks, and out at the tents where they were camping—and some of them, now given the chance, began looking in.

"Rhaim!" she shrieked, and jerked backwards in the bed, trying to get away. We both watched men press their faces up to the windows, trying to see what the glass hid. "Stop!" she said, pushing her free hand out at the window. "Please!" And then she caught her breath and squinted at the men. "They can't see me, can they?"

"No, little moth, they cannot. And if any man ever did, I would send crows to pick out his eyes."

She took a shuddering inhale, gathering herself. "Then what is the meaning of all this?"

"It is only fair. You tortured them with magic—now they should torture you."

She muttered curses I was surprised she even knew, as she flung herself against the mattress in exasperation. "Must everything be a lesson?"

Given that I had limited time to teach her... "Yes."

She groaned. "Can you just not look, then?"

I chuckled darkly, but grabbed the chair and turned around. I made myself comfortable, even though my view of the workers outside was much more disappointing. "You should know by now I'm a quick reader," I warned her, settling in.

I had spent the time it took to modify the cane making a list in my mind of all my responsibilities towards her, to prepare her for a life without me.

This was quite possibly the easiest one to fix.

Because if I died, who would pay for the castle's repairs—and what would be the point, if she couldn't make it fly?

And if Ajeil told a lumber trader down the river, who told someone else, who told yet a third person, about a high-born woman left to her own devices in a decrepit castle in a field —Lisane's freedom would come to an abrupt halt, no matter what she told them her name was.

I heard her inhale and exhale softly. "And you're sure you cannot help?"

The beast of me already envisioned standing, casting my pipe and her chair aside, turning, mounting the bed. *He* did not have to be asked more than once.

Which is why it was good that *he* was not in charge.

I gathered myself before answering her. "No, Lisane. You may need someone to hurt you for your magic, moth, but not for this." From some godlike well deep inside I found the power to put my pipe back into my mouth, take a soothing puff, and ignore the fact that I was so hard it made the rest of me bloodless. "I will read slowly," I told her, "and you may take your time."

24

LISANE

I stared at the back of Rhaim's bowed head, unable to believe it.

I had as much as thrown myself at him, twice now, and for all his talk of possessiveness and crows, this was how he treated me? I gave an exasperated thrash in the bed, against my ties, remembering how I'd first woken up in his castle, with my arms lashed behind me, and everything that'd happened to me since.

"Do you still hate your teacher?" I asked him.

His head rose up as he considered this for a moment. "There's no point in hating the dead."

"Did you kill him?"

"No. But I did think about it often. And he did try to kill me, several times." Rhaim took a draw on his pipe and let out a cloud. "He once set me outside with all my belongings in anger mid-winter. He told me to find another mage to train me; he was through."

"What happened then?"

Rhaim took his pipe from his mouth, rather than keep talking around it. "I slept on his doorstep until I could convince him to let me back in. I would've frozen to death, if I hadn't summoned wolves to sleep with me, for heat's sake. On the fourth day, I don't think he wanted to teach me anymore, so much as he got hungry, and wanted wolf meat, and I was a means to an end."

"Wolf...meat?" I questioned, having never heard of eating such a thing.

"The blizzards that year were endless." I watched him shrug. "Most stories from my past are sad."

And all he wanted me to do was touch myself, I thought, as he went on.

"I'm not particularly pleased about how I was trained, moth, or the methods I've devised to train you. But they were, and are, just means to an end."

Which was why he wasn't over here.

Inside of me.

Because that wouldn't actually be part of my training.

That would mean there was something more between us. Or possibly something less, judging from all the journals I'd read of mages too busy to bother to annotate their conquest's names, and Jelena's attitude towards men.

"You are thinking too hard again. I can tell," he said. "The same thing that stops you from accomplishing this is the same thing that hampers your magic."

I groaned. "Shush. Just—stay there, and close your eyes and don't listen."

"Would you like me to go out into the hall?" he asked, and I could hear the laugh hidden in his voice.

"Yes?" I guessed, angry at myself for giving him any ground—but if this was to be done—"*Yes*. Please. Sir."

"Very well," he said, tucking his book beneath his arm and picking up the chair, his pipe again between his teeth. He didn't even look my way, but I could see the corners of his lips curved up in a smile, as he made his way past me.

The door closed, and I was alone with the workers outside—who had given up on peering in.

I relaxed into my bed with a huff.

Okay. I could do this thing now. *Possibly.* I closed my eyes and still felt foolish...but if I did it, I'd be through.

I *could* lie.

Jelena and Vissa had mentioned that.

But I had a feeling Rhaim would know, and what was more, he had a stupid, awful point.

What was magic but a period of control, before letting go?

I frowned, but brought my fingers against myself, following the same path his tongue had in the tub, and where his hand had just directed me, trying to find the right places that would make me feel the same as he had.

I couldn't lick my fingers, to make my motions smoother, but I could dip them inside myself, and did so, putting slack into the rope. I wasn't very wet yet, and pushing my fingers inside, I wished that my virginity was something I could dig out and throw away—or maybe just give it to someone else. Maybe let Vissa borrow it, for her shard of unicorn horn.

I'd started out wanting to learn magic to defeat the Deathless, to somehow take revenge on them for murdering my mother, and then save the rest of the world—but now I knew if I didn't learn it, I'd never be able to save myself.

So I took a deep breath in and ran the pads of my fingertips over the point above my cunt, as Rhaim had so inelegantly called it, where all things converged, and where I hoped I could touch myself the right way, finally.

I closed my eyes, concentrating, remembering—and now I had more thoughts than just the tub.

There was the power I'd held over Rhaim that night at the tavern. The lost look in his eyes when I'd been crawling to him, and afterward, when I'd licked his hand. The swell of him beneath his leathers, how heavy he'd been when I had pulled him out of them.

That night I *wanted* him. And I was *hungry*.

But if he wasn't going to help me now...I had to help myself.

I scooted lower in the bed, shifting my weight—then I realized I could bend my knees and get even more slack on the rope, to do as I liked. I shifted my hand to touch myself more fully, tracing all of my soft parts, thinking about what it would be like if he were joined with me.

The weight of him above me, my thighs parted wide—the scent of him, musky and male—and the sound of him, saying my name, like he couldn't believe that I was with him.

I bit my lips and ran my free hand over a breast, pulling at a nipple roughly like he'd done in his stable, imagining with all my strength that it was him, not me. I remembered the way he'd looked at me when my mouth was wrapped around him. The harsh sound of his breathing when he stroked himself. What it'd felt like yesterday when he'd been cruel.

I kept replaying moments through my mind until my body caught up, and I could drag enough wetness up from myself to make my fingers slippery. There was a soft spot there, just a little nub, and if I rubbed it right, it reminded me of sunlight and flame, the stars at nighttime, and deep, deep shadow. What it felt like to have a man suck between your legs like he was thirsty and what it felt like to have that same man fist your hair and say, "Don't bite."

Last, I thought of a version of Rhaim my age, handsome, serious, quite possibly sorrowful, sleeping in a den of wolves, shivering, and I wished I could save him from everything else that befell him in his life. I felt sure that that unscarred version of him would've stepped into bed with me gladly.

Maybe he'd be as bad at this as I was.

Maybe we'd have been true magical equals.

And then we'd both be together, here, finding these things out.

I slid my fingers deep, imagining kindnesses that the Rhaim I knew could not bring himself to offer, grinding myself against my palm, as a tension I couldn't deny rose inside my hips. The space between my legs became a dripping, needy mess, clenching around fingers in a way that felt good but didn't quite satisfy until—my hips bobbed beneath my hand of their own accord and I was closer than I'd ever gotten before—*closer—please oh please—please please please please—please!—yes—yes—yesssssss.*

I cried out, I couldn't help myself, lightning shooting through my core, followed by waves of thunderclaps, and me gasping through it all the while, but I bit my lips so I wouldn't shout out his name.

And when I was through, the door opened, and the Rhaim of the now walked in. His expression was unreadable, as he drew his gaze up and down me—I was slightly sweaty and panting, just like a raced horse. He leaned over the bed silently, unlaced my right wrist, and brought my wet fingers to his mouth.

I bit back a groan as I felt him suck my juices off of me, a final quiver running through my body, as he slowly pulled them out again while running his tongue between them, cleaning my skin as I had his. Then he let my hand go and tugged the knots off my ankles. "I will see you tomorrow for training, moth," he said matter-of-factly, like I wasn't naked and my taste wasn't on his tongue.

I licked my own lips and said the only thing I could. "Yes, sir."

I knew it was just dawn after I woke up—there was light streaming through my bedroom windows, my shutters still open to the outside world. I'd fallen asleep right after Rhaim had left my room the prior night, all of my nervous tension wrung out of me by the satisfaction I'd given myself. I wanted to be indolent and lie in bed all day reading—and maybe touch myself again, now that I knew how—except that I knew he'd be expecting me.

And I could still feel the magic his torture had imbued me with sitting inside me, like a fine stack of wood in an unlit fireplace. All that potential...just...waiting.

Maybe touching myself had helped me. Maybe it'd make it easier for me to access it today. Maybe all of Rhaim's lessons weren't as frustrating as they sometimes felt.

I got out of bed and walked over to the windows, wrapping my robe about myself. I could hear the men working outside; it was a miracle I'd slept in as long as I had. They shouted to each other, doing assorted manly things. I could see them out in the field thirty feet below sawing and cooking, measuring and pulling ropes—I could even see one man step away briefly to relieve himself, which made me laugh.

It would've been so lovely, and possibly instructive, to just get to sit in here and watch people all day. Two men briefly blocked my window's view, tromping on nearby scaffolding, carrying beams of wood atop their shoulders. There were ropes that led up carrying bigger beams, too, and a system of pulleys helping to lift them, with a team of horses much like Rhaim's piebald down below. I stepped closer to the window and tried to peer up, trying to see how they were managing on higher floors, but couldn't see very far.

"Lisane!" Finx said from the door, scuttling in. "Rhaim sent me to wake you up. Breakfast is almost ready."

I grinned at the spider-cat as he came up beside me. "Tell him I'll be there in a moment."

Finx bobbed at that. "Thank you for last night. You have no idea what it's been like, to have to listen to them gripe about me all night—and much of the day, too!" He darted to the window and looked out. "So it's true that the outside world doesn't like spiders?"

"Sadly, yes," I told him. "But that's because they've never met you."

"And spiders outside can't talk?" He tilted his body up, so he could look at me with his largest two sets of golden eyes. "Rhaim told me that, but maybe you've met different ones."

"If they can, it's not in a language humans know. They're also not as big as you." I squatted down on my heels beside him, to give his back a scratch. "It's why I was scared of you, initially. But then I learned who you were, and now you're my friend."

Finx thrummed beneath my hand—and then the castle shook. A large cracking sound outside made the two of us startle as men started shouting. Finx threw webbing faster than I could react, aiming for a man who was plummeting from overhead, but it just hit the glass.

"No!" I shrieked, lunging for the window, with both my hands and my mind.

My magic spooled out of me, the same way Finx's webs did, only mine wasn't blocked. I felt it catch hold of the man just outside where I could see—I was yanked forward, and I had to pull back, to try to balance myself, and as I did, I felt the weight of the man and the magic I held both, levering against me, like my hands were being crushed by rocks.

And this time I could see my pain—my hands were red, going fat and purple. It felt like my bones were being ground to dust. I could hear the men outside shout in amazement as tears sprang to my eyes.

How much magic did I have in me? Could I pull him up to safety? I raised my arms up, crying out, as I took a step back, and I could see the bent back of the worker now, hovering in midair.

"Lisane!" Finx said, peering over. "He's floating! Lisane?"

"*Get—Rhaim—*" I gritted out—but he didn't need to.

Rhaim was there.

He thundered past me, going from human to beast in a heartbeat, throwing himself through the window.

It shattered into a million pieces of glass and wood around him as he caught the worker and I felt my magic yanked then snap, both of them falling. I shouted out and ran forward, almost out of the window myself, but they were gone.

"Rhaim!" I shouted—as he and the man both emerged on the ground from a portal.

Rhaim's beast dropped the man roughly, looked up, spotted me, and howled.

It was chaos after that. Men swarmed the one who'd fallen like hungry ants, and they thundered down the scaffolding, shouting blame. Rhaim stepped back, and back again, his eyes just for me. My hands were in agony—but—

It had worked.

I'd done it.

I'd saved that man.

I—I was empty now. I couldn't explain how I felt it—but I'd done enough and—

"Lisane," Rhaim snarled, portaling into the room behind me. I heard the sound of his heavy breathing and turned just as he lunged for me. I panicked, remembering his warning, but there was no room to run. His beast picked me up and I shrieked in surprise, watching him turn back into a man as he held me tight. He spun us both, as I kept my hands above his head safely.

"Don't bite me!" I warned him, but I was laughing, the same as he was now, and Finx was running cheerful circles behind him on the walls.

"Moth! Your magic!" A smile such as I had never seen from him lit up his face—pure delight and sheer joy, for me. It felt like I had been given a rare treasure, and now that it was finally safe to cry, I did, but all my tears were happy.

"She did it!" Finx shouted.

"Did you see?" I asked Rhaim.

"I did!" he exclaimed.

"That was me!" I felt the need to claim the moment. No matter what else befell me on my journey—*I had used my magic to save a man's life.*

"That was you!" Rhaim repeated, setting me down to cup my face in both his hands. He swept my tears away with his thumbs. "I'm so proud of you."

"You are?" I asked, before I could take it back.

There was a moment, where our faces were so close to one another we were breathing one another's air, and nothing that had ever happened before in my life—not even the sensation of the magic that'd just flowed through me—had ever felt so right.

"Of course," he told me. I wanted him to lean in, I was about to rock up—but then he spotted my hands, which I was still holding high, like I was about to loop them around his neck. "Oh, moth—"

"It's all right," I told him, because everything was—or would be. I was with him, and—

He stood up fully to take me in, giving me a head shake. "Come. Let me care for you."

All I could do was nod. "Okay."

And after that he picked me up.

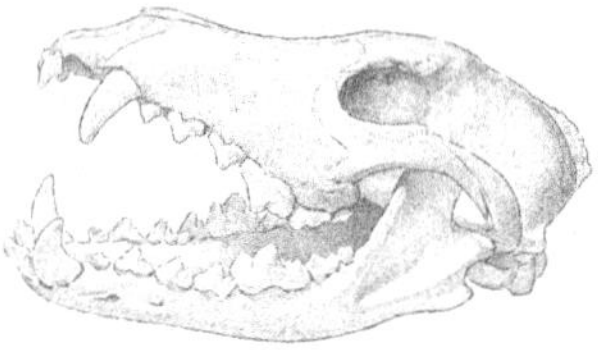

25

RHAIM

Lisane held her hands in front of her this time, instead of wrapping them around my neck, and I could see the damage her magic had done to her—it looked like someone had taken a hammer to them—but she was euphoric from her accomplishment, and also she was healing.

I'd heard the men's shouts from the kitchen, felt the lost beam thump, and my first concern was checking on her—because I felt a great use of magic from nearby—and then...she'd caught the falling man.

Somehow.

Seeing her in pain and striving, I lost control. My beast flowed out of me, to deal with whatever was hurting her as quickly as I could.

And now—I looked down at her. Her eyes were closed, probably dealing with her pain, but her smile was wide and happy. "We should celebrate," I told her. "If you can manage to stay awake tonight."

One of her eyes opened. "If you don't put me to bed, like a recalcitrant child."

I laughed and kicked open the door to the top of my castle, where my healing bath was.

"I already feel a little better, Rhaim," she said.

"Does that mean you're turning down this bath?" I asked, making sure to sound mystified, and she laughed.

"Absolutely not," she said, letting me set her down to stand. Her robe—the same one she'd had on overnight—was wrapped around her, and I could still scent what she'd done last night on her body and injured fingers. She stood with the rising dawn behind her, shining light through wild strands of her hair and the fabric's translucent silk, making her look like some kind of goddess. "But," she began, holding out her hands, "it's true."

I nodded strongly. "The more powerful you get, the faster you'll heal. You just need to trust yourself enough to risk your price. And while I wouldn't ever wish you harm, Lisane, that, back there," I said, pointing, "was glorious."

Her lips went tight as she tried to hold back a smug smile. "It was, wasn't it?" Then she turned to the tub and stepped in. The wet silk clung to her diaphanously, making her appear more naked than actual nudity would've been. I made myself look away, rather than risk temptation—then heard her hiss as her hands sank into the water, and felt a fool. "Thank you," she said.

"Of course. You can stay in the tub as long as you like—"

"Not for this." I glanced down, and found her near the tub's edge, so her body was hidden from me, blurred by her hair streaming beneath the water behind her. "For...everything else."

I squatted down on my heels in front of her. "It will be easier on you if you keep hating me."

She laughed. "Easier on you, more like."

"No. I mean it, Lisane." Now was the time to tell her the truth. All of it. She didn't have magic she could accidentally focus on me...and she deserved to know. I inhaled to begin—and then heard even more shouting from below. *Oh, no*, I thought, feeling a wave of awareness pull at my magic, as Lisane looked past me, concerned. "Fuck," I growled, and stood again. I didn't want any distractions once we started having this conversation.

"Rhaim?" she asked, and rose up from the milky water.

"Stay here." I waved her back. "I'll return shortly. Everything's fine," I lied then portaled.

I returned myself to the ground about a hundred feet from my castle...and into the middle of a bunch of sheep.

"What. The," I growled, looking around. The poor farmer's field my laborers were already ruining was now utterly trampled, as an entire herd made its way in, and Ajeil was arguing with the shepherd—who started waving for my attention the second he saw me.

"Beast Mage! There you are! I was waiting in town, but then I heard you were out here instead, and I thought—"

"Go back." I pointed my finger back on the road he'd come in on. But it was too late. All the people and beasts who'd been waiting for me at the well had changed their destinations. There was a long trail of livestock trampling into the field from the road, and then on the road for as far as the eye could see.

"This is a worksite!" Ajeil was shouting, trying to wave the oncoming wall of creatures back.

It had been days since I'd seen the outside of my castle, but they were almost finished with the external structure—I'd only needed a few more days of peace. Half of the people present were coming to talk to me; the other half were gawking at Lisane's window, which Finx was industriously sealing up with webs. They couldn't see into my castle from the ground, but they could see him at work.

"Is that a spider?" a new voice shrieked from below, pointing up, and their exclamation was echoed by others who spotted him.

Ajeil came over quickly. "I'm so sorry, sir. Thank you for saving my man—"

"How soon can you finish?" I asked flatly.

"Another three days. Round the clock. I won't forget what you did for Relph—he's my wife's cousin—and I know we owe you a new window."

I shook my head, not at him, but at the whole situation, as people crowded us, shoving their animals in front of them, a cacophony of creatures bleating, lowing, crowing.

"Stop," I said in a dangerous tone. But not all of them heard me, or if they did, they were too self-absorbed. "I said, stop!" I shouted, and released a wave of energy, directed at all of their animals. The sheep stopped mid-step, horses froze, and geese mid-flight glided to the ground and then stayed where they landed.

The only motion left was from the people, who I couldn't control—I saw Lisane's little friend from the tavern, dropping down from the back of a stilled horse to run over, looking at the castle in awe, and then at the surrounding men, like one of them might be hiding Lisane.

"I told you all I would return," I said, now that I had the group's attention.

"It's been two days, sir!" someone shouted, and others agreed with him.

A man took out a handkerchief from somewhere on his person and blew his nose with it. "And to be fair to us—that's also what you said, thirty years ago."

I closed my eyes and tried to defuse the violence in my heart. "Go back to town. I'll be there tomorrow, for a span of two more days."

"But we already drove our flocks out 'ere, sir!" complained another man.

"And *I* will drive them to the ends of the earth, where *you* will never see them again, if you don't comply with my direction. Go. Back," I snarled, letting some of my beast through. I should've known this would happen—every day longer here was risking it. "Go back or I will fly my castle away now, and you will *never* see me again."

"Hey, hey, hey!" Ajeil shouted, for their attention, making waving motions with his hands, trying to scatter them. "What are you all, daft? Don't make him angry!"

Men and women and the children that they'd hauled out here with them to help channel beasts grumbled, but began to disperse, which would've been fine, except for the fact that there were still who knew how many people and beasts already on their way out here, churning the road beneath their hooves—and not all of those incoming had heard me, and they probably wouldn't accept hearing it secondhand...

I portaled into my bedroom, scooped up handfuls of gold and gemstones from one of my many piles, and poured it into a bag, returning to the ground outside to throw it at Ajeil. He caught it, his eyes wide, and then he sighed, knowing what it meant.

"Give the green stones in there to Pella, and the small red stone to her dark-haired servant girl."

"All-Beast," he began, apologetically.

"Someone else will finish my repairs. Thank you for your work so far. Pull your men back, and undo whatever hooks hold your scaffolding to my home, if you want to keep that wood."

"Perhaps my son will see you someday?" he asked.

"Perhaps. But also, perhaps not. Grandson, maybe."

He put his hand out, and I took it to shake, then portaled back to my roof, only to find Lisane out of the tub and peering over one of the crenelations. She was bent over it at hip height, her perfect ass high in the air, hidden only by sheer wet silk. "Why are they all here?" she asked, noticing me without turning around, with her magic—so naturally that she didn't even realize that she'd done it. My pleasure at that staved off my erection for a crucial moment, allowing me to control myself.

"Because of me. What of your hands?"

"They're much better," she said, smiling as she turned, holding one out. "I didn't disbelieve you about the healing, Rhaim, but I have to admit I was scared it might not work for me."

"Your magic is in you now. No one can ever take it away from you."

"Lirane!" a girl's voice shouted up from below, instantly regaining my moth's attention. She leaned over and waved back.

"Jelena!" she shouted cheerfully, then looked to me. "Is there someplace safe in the castle I could show her?"

"No. We're leaving."

She blinked. "What? Why?"

"Due to that mess down there." From the castle's higher vantage, I could see the oncoming livestock spilling across the road for miles.

"But the workers—"

"There are other workers. In other towns. You will find girls to befriend there—"

"But—Rhaim—I like it here—"

"Only because you know no better." She gave me a betrayed look as I went on. "I came here to tell you, moth. Not to ask for your opinion."

"Just—one more day?" she pleaded, and when met with my adamant silence, shifted to frustration. "Let me go say goodbye at least!"

"The longer we wait, the worse it will get." I knew from experience. "First they complain—then they throw rocks."

"And the great All-Beast is afraid of a few stones?"

I snorted. "No. But the great All-Beast does know his own temper."

Then I felt something I had hoped to indefinitely avoid—a sensation like someone was drawing claws across my magic.

I heard creatures begin to call out in panic and men curse my name in misplaced blame.

Deathless were near.

"What is that?" Lisane breathed, feeling it as well.

I let half of my beast out and watched her eyes widen. "Get inside. *Stay inside,*" I commanded with his rough voice, then portaled to the ground.

The animals outside my castle possessed the sense the people didn't, beginning to stampede away, bucking or flying for their freedom.

"Bring my sheep back at once!" a shepherd accosted me before his common sense caught up with him and his jaw dropped.

"YOU ALL NEED TO GO!" I snarled, shouting at full volume, wheeling myself in a circle, hoping I could frighten them away if nothing else. "NOW! IT IS NOT SAFE FOR YOU HERE."

None of these people had weapons—but I couldn't help them. The longer I stayed, the more likely it was I'd get caught here by Jaegar's men. "GO!" I bellowed, dropping to all fours to chase after the closest group of them, who'd apparently lost the capacity to think while gawking at me. I gave up on words and snarled and bayed to make them leave.

Then shrieks began—not from nearby. The ground shifted, and it was too late. Dirt erupted in a cloud, sending the people standing atop it to their knees, which meant they were underfoot when the first Deathless crawled out of the ground.

I stood for a moment, transfixed by two opposite desires—to help the helpless townspeople here, and to steal Lisane away to safety and not look back.

And then she was there, racing up to me, barefoot in the grass, her wet dress still clinging to her. "Rhaim! What is happening?" But it only took her a moment to absorb it all in, the foul creatures lumbering out of the ground, the way the ones nearest people had already brought them to their knees and were devouring them. I saw all the blood drain from her face, her jaw drop with horror, and her presence there decided me. I swept her up. I had to keep her safe, it was more important than anything—

"Let me down!" she shouted, beating at my chest. "Rhaim!"

"We're leaving—"

"No!" She squirmed in my arms to get free—it only made me hold her tighter. "We have to help!"

"People are replaceable, moths are not!" I said, yanking the first door to my castle open and shoving her inside. But then I heard fresh screams. "Fuck," I growled. "Fuck!" I slammed the door to my castle shut, trapping her inside, and then raced around, batting away the slow ill-moving bodies of the dead. "Run!" I howled for anyone who would listen and then loped to pick up two more of the eyeless creatures, snapping at one, and clawing the other, destroying both of them on impact.

Some of the workers had stayed to fight, and some townspeople were thunderstruck, but most of them were now following their livestock, racing away, with the Deathless shambling after—except for some few that'd managed to down a cow, and were feasting on its innards with their sharp teeth. I swept through this group easily, as they were all distracted, but another small herd of them was coming for me, with more pouring out from behind. I could stave them off long enough for all the remaining townspeople to get away, but I knew there were too many of them for me to fully stop—and the more magic I burned through, the more danger my moth would be in when I was finished.

I couldn't abandon her for days to regain myself—nor could I be trusted with my beast around her, either.

I raced from monster to monster, disemboweling them, ripping out throats, tearing them in two, shaking off arms that grabbed me even though their owners were gone.

"Run away," I told the few remaining brave workers, in a voice even deeper than my own. *He* was here, he wanted to ride me, and then claim his prize. I needed to get inside my castle, *now*, and take off, and lock myself in my portal chamber until I was sane.

Then I heard my moth's voice from above. "Rhaim!" she shouted, from up in her window, where she was tearing through the webbing window Finx had created. She leapt out onto the scaffolding and started running down the planks.

Things in me that were not good lurched forward, just like the Deathless from their graves. "Lisane," I growled, with what was left of man in me, begging her to see me and to understand. "Go—now—*go*—"

This time she stopped just out of reach. "I want to help."

"Your father's men ...will be here soon," I managed to get out.

"But they're not here now," she said, coming closer, stretching out one newly healed hand. "Rhaim, let me help you."

From this close her scent was overwhelming, almonds and honey, shining and clean—but I wanted her to smell like me.

I gnashed my teeth at her and raced behind us both, slaughtering more of the slow creatures, feeling myself slip away like hourglass sand. I crushed three of the things at once, and then stood up to wheel toward her, the fur of my chest painted with their blood, the hot hard rod of my shaft pushing out of its sheath.

"You told me to trust myself. I do. And I also trust you," she said, taking another step forward.

It was too late. I was broken. *He* grabbed for her and pulled her in, spinning her so that her back was against his chest and he could throw her on the ground to fuck. "You shouldn't," he growled, the words thick in his mouth as he grabbed her hair and yanked her neck sideways. "You are no tamer of beasts," he said, as he opened up his mouth, and he bit her.

26

LISANE

I screamed—from surprise, and because it hurt. Rhaim's fangs sank into my shoulder and neck, front and back, his teeth grinding against my bones, my blood spilling out, dyeing Finx's silk red. The horror of it made me disassociate instantly.

He'd bit me.

He was still biting me.

I could hear the snarls of his beast in my ear, feel his claws as they sank into my skin, and the threat of his heavy flesh behind me. He shook his head, worrying his jaws closer together, making savage sounds, as I cried out.

But in me...

"Rhaim," I breathed, in a warning. Whereas every time I'd ever been filled before it'd been like raindrops into a bucket, I felt power thudding into me now, like crashing waves. I managed to free my far hand and raise it up across my body, to run one finger up against the grain of the fur on his muzzle. "Rhaim, come back."

Then the Deathless finally reached him—and it seemed the only thing more intolerable to him than my freedom was being interrupted. He let go of my shoulder with a wet smack, and more blood flowed, pouring out of the holes he'd left, his muzzle was spattered with it. He took me in, snarled, and then leapt into the fray, killing everything he touched.

Except for me.

I pressed a hand to my wound, feeling woozy enough to pass out, but I was full of power now, so much it felt like burning. It felt like I needed to use it or I really would catch fire.

One of the Deathless had gotten by earlier, and was walking across the field, chasing after the distant sheep. I ran after it, holding my injured arm with the other, trying to ignore the way each step sent jolts of pain. I wasn't sure what I'd do when I caught up; I just knew I needed to do *something*. It was the same reason I couldn't just hide inside the castle.

The last time I'd been forced to hide from the Deathless, I'd been helpless, and I'd lost my mother.

But I wasn't helpless anymore.

The creature heard me coming and slowly turned around. It was naked like the rest of them, its face slack yet puffy, no nose, no eyes, just a mouth full of fang-like teeth. It started coming for me and I backed up.

Surely my magic wouldn't fail me now.

Surely.

I raised my hand, bracing for how much my magic would hurt me, and preparing to let it flow through me nonetheless. And then I tripped, falling on my ass in trampled grasses, yelping as my shoulder bounced.

The Deathless loomed with his eyeless face—and Rhaim was sailing overhead, his beast easily taking down the creature. He rose up, snarled at me, and then looked over my shoulder and kept snarling. I twisted to see behind myself, where things had only gotten worse. The fissure in the ground had widened and more of the creatures had clambered up and out.

I had to close that up somehow...I started running for it with only half an idea in my head and Rhaim racing close behind.

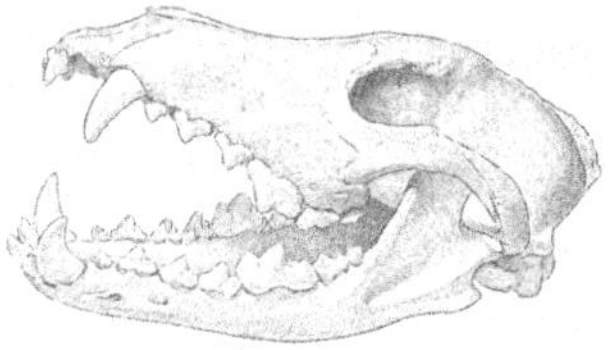

27
RHAIM

He chased after her.

Just like he'd always wanted to.

Except for now, he had competition, the Deathless she dodged turning to follow her, and more arrowing forward from their ranks. He raced around, beside, in front, forced to clear her path so he could keep her safe enough for later, howling his anger the whole time.

All he wanted was the girl, alone. He'd been so close to her in the library, and this was like then, he was every bit as covered in gore, and pleased to feel his well-used muscles burning. He inhabited his form, feeling alive, so close to being free. All he had to do was shepherd her through her current madness, killing the sad-human things around them that broke easily—and then keep running after her. He gnashed at her heels, wishing he could sink his teeth into her tendons, or bite the backs of her thighs, so she couldn't crawl away. Now that he'd tasted her sweet flesh, her blood washing away the monstrous dankness of the other creatures, he knew he'd never get enough. When these foul things were gone, bitten, broken, exploded, sent back into the darkness from which they came, when it was just him, and her, and the purity of the hunt—there would be nothing in his way.

And no one would be able to stop him.

She pulled up short in front of the hole gaping into the earth that the Deathless were clawing out of, and he bellowed his anger at them for delaying his conquest.

One of the creatures came for her, and he swatted it aside, and then pounced on another and shook it, and then gutted a third—

"Rhaim!" she shouted. *He* didn't answer to that name, but he understood her tone. "Move!"

Breathing hard after fighting, and full of anticipation, he moved aside, pacing behind her, watching her raise both her hands. There was a feeling in the air, one opposite to the energy of the Deathless arising, like the pause in the eye of a storm, and then—

She slammed her hands out in front of her, and *he* felt a wave. The air moved and the ground shook, and she was thrown back right at his feet.

But in front of them both the ground shifted, reknitting, dropping to be level, and trapping the remaining Deathless outside.

He bayed his triumph and set about killing the last of them, happily racing from living corpse to living corpse, putting an end to their mockery of life, and when he was finished, he came back to where he'd left her. She was curled up in a ball at his feet.

"Get up, girl-thing," he told her, scratching at her with a paw, and then nosing her forcefully with his muzzle. "Run from me, that I might chase you."

Her delicate eyelids fluttered open, but he could tell she wasn't seeing him, her copper eyes were distant. "My head hurts, Rhaim." She reached an arm up for him, and he went to snap it, putting all his teeth against her, stopping only at the last moment. "Take me home?" she asked, her voice a lost whisper.

If he broke her now...she'd never run.

And that was what he needed.

To hunt, to find, to catch, to fuck.

She wasn't terrified of him right now—and wouldn't be, even if he bit her.

He let her go, stalked around her in a wary circle, then he stood and picked her up.

28

LISANE

Things happened.

I drifted in and out of consciousness for them, only barely aware of what was going on.

Me in Rhaim's tub with him, skin to skin, him holding me against his chest, while he carefully brought handfuls of water up to pour onto my head to help my overheated mind. The sound of his voice as he read to me—I didn't remember any of the words; I just felt the comfort of knowing he was near. Him spooning careful sips of broth into my mouth, and him cleaning me, dressing me, brushing my hair...

I had no idea how much time had passed when I woke. I was in his bedroom, on his bed, propped up on plush pillows, all the covers tucked in. The room was lit with scattered candlelight, and Rhaim was on the far side of the bed, half of him sitting in a chair, the other half spilled towards me, his torso and his arms strewn out on the bed as he slept. There were dark circles under his eyes, and his beard's shadow was longer than I'd ever seen it before.

I reached for him without thinking, ran my fingers into his hair, and tugged.

It took a moment for him to wake up, but when he saw me, the way he looked at me then, all hope and heat—I knew he was mine for life.

"Welcome back, little moth," he said softly.

I blinked at him and smiled, then used his hair to pull him near. "Rhaim," I whispered, as he rose up and crawled close atop the sheets to me. He closed his eyes and set his forehead to mine, smelling like pipe smoke and promises. I wrapped my arms around his neck without question, my eyes welling up with tears that didn't quite race free.

"How do you feel?" he asked when he lifted up.

Now that he was here, with me, like this? My eyes traced every contour of his face, the slope of his cheeks, the hard line of his jaw, his noble nose, and the scar that I had given him. "Whole."

He set his forehead to mine again for a long moment, just breathing. “I thought I’d lost you.”

I rubbed my fingers on the nape of his neck. “Don’t you know that’s impossible?”

“I didn’t dare to dream.” He pulled up and shook his head slowly. “When I bit you, Lisane—”

“I needed you to. To empower me.”

“That doesn’t mean it was right.”

“We’re both still alive though, aren’t we? And—my magic—it worked?”

There was a rumble in his chest. “It did.”

My heart sped up just being near him—in his room, in his bed, beside him, where I belonged. “Then let us both be here, Rhaim.”

I was only afraid he’d deny me for a second, but then he leaned in and asked, “May I show you how to kiss, little moth?”

“Yes,” I whispered. “Please.”

He moved higher on the bed with both his elbows, holding himself over me, and drew the line of his nose along the line of mine, before our lips brushed, and his pulled at the edges of mine softly, as if investigating them, until my mouth naturally opened to give him more access. One of his hands slid beneath my head to hold my hair and keep me still as he pressed his tongue in and I gasped in surprise at the connection, at having part of him in me at last. He lifted his head again like he was trying to read my eyes, and then came back, his tongue pushing in deeper while his lips stayed on mine, and I moaned. I sent my own tongue searching back, my own lips pushing, and heard him growl as his fingers tightened in my hair, both of us trading this moment that we'd fought for back and forth, permission to finally know each other like this, permission to finally admit we cared.

I kept one hand wrapped around his neck, my fingers in his hair, curled against his scalp, and sent the other roving down his back and body, drawing him to me. I wanted his weight above me, in me, moving—I'd never needed anything so badly.

But he kept kissing my mouth like he was drinking from me, pressing in deeply only to retreat and leave me pining, bereft. It felt like he was pulling the spirit from my body, leaving me an empty shell in his wake, dying to be made full.

"Rhaim," I whispered when I couldn't take it any longer, and he started kissing elsewhere, licking and sucking at my jaw, down the soft skin of my neck, the hollow of my throat. "Oh —Rhaim—"

He made a pleased sound back at me, nuzzling into where my neck met my shoulder with his face, so I could feel his kiss and the scrape of his beard. I pushed down the sheets, trying to give myself over, breathing hard, and he rose up above me, his pupils dark as coals, as he reached for his shirt. I grabbed my dress to shimmy upwards, wanting to be naked too, and when he was done with his shirt, he helped me tug my dress up till I was free.

"Little moth," he murmured, moving forward as I fell back until he was holding himself above me, lowering himself from his hands to his elbows as he sank to kiss my breasts. My jaw dropped as his mouth found the same nipple he'd threatened to pierce. I ran both my hands into his hair as he sucked it. Waves of anticipation rolled through my body like his tongue controlled my hips.

"Sir," I whispered, and felt him chuckle.

"Yes, little moth," he said, pulling himself off of my breast indulgently, having teased it into a pebbled peak, before starting on the next one. "Give all your sirs to me," he commanded, but in moments all I could do was moan.

Everywhere he touched me was perfect...perfectly torturous.

Because I needed.

I wanted.

I ached.

"Rhaim," I called for him and rocked my hips with something akin to panic. I had to feel him in me; I had to feel us fit together. He made a commensurate sound of pleasure, and then pushed himself up, yanking the rest of the sheets away and sending his hands to the laces of his leathers.

My eyes were half-lidded with desire, and all I could do was nod and keep nodding as his heavy cock fell free.

"I will be so careful with you, Lisane," he promised, finishing pushing off his leathers, until we were both naked at long last—and then his hands reached for the head of his cock, twisting open and unlacing the thick metal ring that hung there, and tossing it aside, as he picked up a bottle from a nearby bookshelf.

"What if I don't want you to be?" I breathed.

"Then I would tell you to be careful what you ask for." He waited a measured moment, watching me, then took himself in hand, decanting slow-pouring fluid along his shaft, and then I watched him fuck his hand, same as he had my hands move over him at the tavern that night, rolling his sheath back and forth along his thick length, until all of him was slick and shiny.

Watching him do that did things to me I had never felt before. I was full of some raw, animalistic urge at the sight of it, and thought maybe he would need his magic to tame me.

"Roll on your side, little moth," he said, as he put the bottle down. I was blinking back to reality when he added, "Do as you're told." I shifted in his bed to do so, not sure what was coming next, and he laid himself behind me. He wrapped one arm beneath me, and his thick length rubbed against my ass as he started kissing me again, behind my neck, beneath my ear, then hoarsely whispered, "I'm not going to deflower you tonight, Lisane. I'm going to fuck your ass instead."

I stiffened, hoping I hadn't heard him right, and turned far enough within his arms to see his face. "What?"

"You heard me." And I could tell from his tone that his mind wouldn't be changing.

"But—but that is all I want!" I protested, rocking back against him. "Please, Rhaim, I'm dripping," I pleaded.

"I know, moth, I smell it," he said, his voice rough and low. "And I am dripping too. But I need to show you something first, and this is the only way to do it safely."

"I don't understand," I pouted.

"Trust me, and you will."

And now I frowned. "The last time I trusted you, you bit me."

The expression on his face then was complicated. "I told you not to trust my beast. And you healed," he said simply.

I looked away from him then, curling into the bed, and he pulled me to his chest.

"Little moth, whether you knew it or not, your entire life has been bent around what lies in between your legs: were you safely hidden, were you pure, could you go quietly to a man? But I want all the rest of you, your mind, your heart, your soul," he said, punctuating each statement with lingering kisses, on my shoulder, my collarbone, and the nape of my neck. "And my desires for your body...are far less wholesome." The way he said it made me swallow in anticipation. "Every night I take myself in hand and dream of pumping into you," he confessed. "I imagine you in front of me, above me, below me, in all sorts of ways, speared by my cock, me fucking you unto shuddering." He'd stopped his kisses, and now his words were in a heated rush as he rocked his hips against mine. "All I long for is the sweet sound of your release, the sirs you will give me when you scream."

"Then take me, Rhaim," I whispered, in no way above begging.

The hand wrapped around me plucked at a nipple, while the other reached and slid between my cheeks to rub at my tighter hole with a slicked finger. "I will, little moth—but this way first, and then all the others." I made a whining sound at him, and he chuckled in dark amusement. "Don't worry, given half a chance after this, I will take your flower so often that I'll have a grand bouquet."

I huffed. "It's not funny," I complained, and he made a demurring sound.

"Have I ever done anything to you without good reason?" he asked, and that made me stiffen.

"No...sir," I reluctantly admitted.

"Then do you think you can trust me a little bit longer?" he asked, pressing his finger in slightly. He had my full attention. I was afraid, and somewhat unhappy, but he'd never hurt me accidentally.

No, any time he'd hurt me, he'd had a calculating purpose.

I nodded slowly.

"Good," he purred. "So let me in to you, where I belong," he said, and started spiraling his finger in.

I closed my eyes, dizzy in an instant, even more so when he took my earlobe into his mouth and sucked. It was cruel how wet I was, and how that wetness was wasted, as he worked his way into a place I'd never even considered allowing anything entrance before.

"I will make you feel good, moth," he swore, kissing my neck again. "I'll be so careful. So slow." His words kept a rhythm with his finger stretching me, playing in and out. "You pant so prettily."

I hadn't even realized that I had been, but I was. "It's—new—" I said, and I wasn't sure it was a complaint anymore, as I started to relax.

"I know," he said, before licking up the shell of my ear. "Everything with you is." I gave a soft gasp at that, which he took the wrong way. "Let me know if you need more oil."

I shook my head quickly. "It just feels wrong, is all."

"It does, a little," he agreed. "But then after that, I promise it will feel right," he said, sliding more of his finger inside my ass. I let out a breathy moan, feeling him work himself there, back and forth, spiraling out, tension building and then releasing each time he shifted.

"Rhaim," I whispered, and started rocking.

"See, moth?" he asked, and I felt him roll his hips, the fat head of his cock nudging against my legs. "Open up your legs a little. I want to put another finger in."

I did as I was told, I curled my head against his arm and my pillow, and made a helpless noise at being entered. In an instant I was being stretched tight again...until he worked me looser, pulling and rubbing, showing me it was safe to give myself over. I felt full at the same time I felt hungry, beginning to moan in the same time as the thrusts of his hand.

Rhaim kissed my shoulder and back, the corner of my jaw, and his other hand on my chest plumped my breast, all the while he kept playing with me, teasing me, murmuring delicious things, about how brave I was, how sweet, how lovely.

I had one knee splayed out and my ass tilted up for him, my face pressed along his arm, making soft sounds, whimpering as he sped up.

"Pretty, maybe," I protested. "And brave—yes." He had three fingers pumping in me now, and I drew my teeth against his bicep, hissing and feeling full. "But sweet?"

"Compared to me," he laughed. I laughed too, and then he pounced on me, his mouth to mine, pressing me into the bed, kissing me roughly as his fingers withdrew. I made a lost sound at the sudden emptiness, but I knew it wouldn't last for long, as I cast a heavy-lidded gaze behind myself to see him wipe his fingers on the bed and then take himself in hand anew.

"Little moth," Rhaim said, his voice going low in warning, "I have to have you." He held himself up with one hand as he stroked himself with the other, and clear fluid dripped from the tip of him, same as oil had from the bottle.

"Good," I told him. "Because I am as I have been for quite some time, sir."

His hand paused, and he tilted his head. "And what's that?"

"Yours."

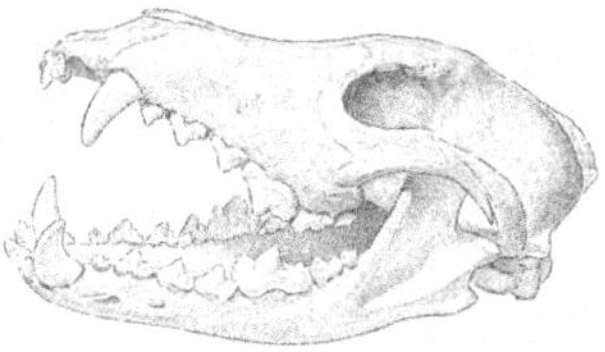

29

RHAIM

Hearing that almost set me loose upon her, and I didn't know how I could live overwhelmed by these twin desires: wanting to fuck her into the ground, and wanting to protect her with my life.

I made a wild sound and went back to the mattress behind her, grabbing her wrist with my oil-slicked hand, bringing it back to grab me.

"You know where I am going—line me up."

She gave a soft whine of complaint. "Making me complicit? Again?"

"No, moth." I chuckled. "I just want your hand wrapped around me."

She squeezed me gently at that, and started rubbing her asshole with the head of my cock. I'd prepared her as best I could, but there was no denying that this was her first time, and that I was large. I was glad I'd taken my jewelry out. "Tell me when you're ready," I whispered.

I saw her nod and mouth the word, "Now."

I rolled my hips up, feeling her tight ring of muscle start to make a sucking O. I bowed my head into her shoulder with a hiss, then paused, pushing barely in and hardly out, feeling her hand still stroke me. "Can you take more, moth?"

She nodded again, and I rose up to use her hair to hold her still and kiss her, feeling her body relax against me as I pushed. She whimpered into my mouth and then moaned as the head of my cock settled into her, the heat inside her inviting more of me in. I pulled back, sure my eyes were as lost as hers were. "You feel so good, Lisane."

In response to that, she rocked, and breathed my name. "Rhaim—"

"Yes, moth?" I asked, kissing the point of her shoulder, rolling her nipple as I held her breast, and still carefully pushing.

"It's just—" she said, and then lost her words, as I slipped in another finger-width. "I feel—"

"Stop thinking so hard," I growled softly from behind her. "It's like magic, moth. It doesn't have to make sense. Let it all go and just be here." She whined again at that, and I continued. "I like the way you feel, little moth," I said, and licked the delicate shell of her ear. "Inside and out. I like your soft skin," I said, trailing a hand down her flank. "Your smooth skin," I said, pushing two fingers on either side of her pussy. "And your places with hair," I said, grabbing hold of the light curls that were just above her clit. "I like the way you smell when you're clean, and your scent when you're dirty," I pushed myself further into her with each phrase, then paused so she'd know I'd gained that ground. "I like the way you taste, the salt of your sweat, your tart juices, and your sweet, delicious tears." I brought my hand back up to catch her jaw and make her look at me. "I want all of you, Lisane. Every single piece of you belongs to me, and I will have it."

"You will," she agreed, just as lost now as she had been when I was whipping her.

"My poor little blissed-out moth," I said, grinning wickedly. "Put your fingers into your cunt and feed me your honey."

She took a deep breath at that, as if resurfacing from the depths. Then she bit her lips and put her hand between her legs, bringing her wet fingers back to me. I took her wrist and held her still as I licked them.

"You're such an animal, Rhaim," she whispered.

"You say that like it's a bad thing." I mock snarled and pretended to bite her fingertips. Then I pulled her wrist down to the small of her back. "But if I truly were," I warned her, breathing roughly in her ear. "There'd be nothing to stop me from fucking you."

I felt the effect my words had on her body, as she gave me a perfect sound of submission. Her pupils went wider, her head rolled back, her body rocked down, and her ass rose up, offering everything to me.

"Fuck, little moth," I whispered harshly, grabbing her hips and leaning forward. "I'm going to fit into you. I'm going to get all the way." I kept her wrist crushed between us, trapped as I took hold of the sheets by her shoulders, just giving her enough room to breathe below me as I started to rut. "I need you, Lisane," I grunted, only barely controlled. "I need you to take me—" And then I was there. Hilt deep in her, my balls slapping against her flooded cunt—she gasped and I knew she felt it too.

I wanted to howl my triumph over her; I wanted to bite her savagely again, only this time with my human teeth. She was mine, my moth, my Lisane, and woe be to anyone who would ever try to take her from me. The fate I had doled out to Vethys would be a small thing compared to what I would do to others now that I had felt her spread beneath me. I would never give her up, and anyone who tried to take her had to die.

She was breathing hard, and I remembered my promise to take her slowly. I lowered myself to gently kiss her cheek.

“I’m so full,” she whispered.

“I know,” I told her. I was tempted to wrap my arm around her and put the heel of my hand on her belly, to see if I could feel the head of my cock inside.

“I’ve never felt this way before,” she went on.

“Me either,” I answered honestly, and then she turned, trying to look up with a betrayed pout.

“Don’t joke.”

“I’m not. I’ve been in other people, yes, but it’s never been like this for me.”

“Why not?” she asked.

I fell to one elbow to stare into her eyes. “Maybe because they weren’t you.”

The look she gave me then was soulful but tinged with sorrow. “You say pretty things, but do you mean them?”

I smoothed her hair back with my other hand. “Let me show you.”

30

LISANE

Rhaim moved to let my trapped hand go and wound my fingers with his own, pressing my palm into the sheets before catching my other to do the same. Then he moved to kiss me as he rocked, pushing my hips into the bedding like we were doing a profane dance.

I moaned, so full of him, stretched taut and knees spread wide. I'd had no idea how this would feel till he was in me, but now—I liked it. All of it. Him looming over me, how he'd worked his way inside, the way he was now pressed deep. The sound of his harsh breathing in my ear, the scent of my need, and my own taste mirrored back to me on his lips.

I bowed my head into his bedding and did my best to lift my hips up.

"*Fuck*, Lisane," he grunted, surging into me. I made a wild sound as his balls slapped me, relishing their impact on the place that he'd once licked.

"More, sir," I pleaded.

He growled rather than answer as he sped up, and dropped his head to be next to mine. "My sweet little virgin moth," he said, one word per thrust. "Who once wanted to fight me—who now takes my cock."

"Yes," I moaned.

He let go of my hands and folded one arm beneath me to cup my breast, and sent the other below me entirely to rub between my legs. I gasped to feel him there, playing with me, working his fingertips in quick little circles. Then he growled and pulled us both to one side again. "Hold your leg up, give me space." I did as I was told and started crying out, deep, low moans I'd never heard from myself before as he took me, and he gave an appreciative growl. "Keep making those noises, moth. You fucking sound like you're in heat."

Because...it felt like I was? If I was, then all of this would make so much more sense. How everything he did to me felt like something that I needed. How I felt like I was about to explode from all the pressure building up.

His hand slid up from my breast to circle my throat. "My little moth's going to come so hard. I can feel it winding up.

And the second you come, Lisane, I'll come too, I'll plunge my cock in you and fill you." He was breathing harder, his hips slowing down, only to thrust into me more sharply. "I can't wait to feel you coming around me. I need to feel your ass squeeze me tight."

Coming...was the perfect word for it. It wasn't the past, it wasn't the future; it was just a perpetual state of being. The act of acting, of having something done to you and doing it to someone else, a tangled-up word that caught at the edges of what it meant to be put into motion, hurtling toward a promise of relief.

"Rhaim," I whispered, my stomach clenching, my ass too, all of me on the verge. "Rhaim," I hissed, and felt him growl and shove himself deep. "Rhaim!" I shouted, and started to thrash, my hips beating against his in their own time. "Oh —*sir!*—fuck—Rhaim!" It sounded like I was begging him and maybe I was, because I didn't want it to ever stop.

And it didn't feel like he did, either. His cock took me in short, rough thrusts, one of his hands clutched around my throat, the other at my pulsing pussy, while the sounds he made behind me built up and then he roared, pulsing forward, spearing hard, snarling, and then pulling back with a groan.

"Lisane," he murmured as I kept shivering with little snaps of delight, unable to come up with words. And he kept moving, slower now, more carefully, like he wanted to keep exploring this shared space between us, unable to think of leaving.

I nuzzled myself back into him, dazed and breathless.

"Give me your hand," he commanded.

I let go of the sheets I was holding and limply obeyed. He took it and brought it behind my back, to the same part of his cock that I'd held earlier when I'd aimed it. "This is what I wanted to show you, moth," he whispered in my ear.

I didn't understand at first; there was too much blood rushing in my ears, but when I couldn't wrap my hand around him I finally understood.

"That's my knot, moth," he said quietly. "If I'd taken your slick cunt with it, I wouldn't have been able to thwart temptation—it would be in you, and you'd be locked to me."

My lips parted in surprise. "Locked? For how long?"

"For a short while." He kissed my temple. There was a long pause, and then he added, "You holding it feels better than you will ever know."

I twisted to look up at him. "I wish I had some way of trapping you to me."

"You do not need a leash to keep me," he said, kissing me softly, before giving me a bittersweet smile. "I promise I am yours."

"For how long?" I asked, though I didn't like the quaver in my tone.

"Until my dying breath, little moth, or for however long you want me."

I reached up to play my fingertips against his lips, and trace the outline of his jaw. "And what if I want you for forever?"

He bowed his head to mine and breathed. "Then even when the end happens, it will come too soon."

We lay there together in the echoes of our contentment, and now that I could touch Rhaim without repercussions, I wanted to. He knew so much more of me than I of him. I moved to twist toward him more fully, but he stopped me, saying, "You'll make a mess. I have filled you to the brim." He pulled up the sheet from below us and pushed it between my legs as he pulled out. It might've been embarrassing if he hadn't spent the past who knew how many days taking care of me.

I wound the sheet between my legs and turned, finally getting to look at him, naked and relaxed. I touched the scars on his chest, the one on his arm that he wouldn't let me sew, and finally I placed my hand over his heart again, where his mage-mark was, finding it a perfect match for my palm and fingers.

"Fitting," he said quietly, watching me with heavy-lidded eyes, patiently tolerating my attention.

"How long has it been since you've truly slept?" I asked, reaching to pull the stubble of his beard. "Don't lie."

He gave a low chuckle. "Too long."

"Then sleep for me. I'll go bathe and then come back." I kissed him, then carefully wriggled for the edge of the bed.

"Here, moth," he said, I first thought to offer me something, but then realized it was a command.

"Back here," I promised, and watched him nod, even though his eyes were drifting shut.

"My door will never be closed to you again."

"That's wise," I told him, leaning forward briefly. "Because I don't know if you heard, but—I know magic."

His eyes were fully closed, but one of his eyebrows still rose as half his lips lifted into a smirk. "Did you want a bath, or a spanking?"

I laughed, and ran off.

I came back clean, with several extra towels, and after a detour to my bedroom, all my extra bedding. I brought all these back to Rhaim's room, and found him as I'd left him, sleeping peacefully on his bed.

He was handsome to me when he was awake, but he looked younger now. In sleep, there wasn't concern at the edges of his eyes, or worries that crossed his brow.

And I couldn't fully believe that he was for me.

He was an entirely other person, with his own thoughts and dreams and inclinations, and yet somehow he had chosen me as thoroughly as I had chosen him. It was exhilarating but also strange—like I'd woken up from my magical stupor and gained a new appendage.

Or a pet.

I hid my smile behind my hand, considering my massive beast of a man, who ate both meat and me, drawing one of my sheets up and across his scar-covered back. Half of the candles in his room had gone out in my absence, and I blew out the rest of them, not wanting us both to sleep near an open flame, cupping just a little light inside my hand to see by.

Finding magic had been like finding him, and now they were inextricably linked inside me—and just as magic had made a space inside me, he had too. My feelings for him were every bit as palpable inside me for me as my magic was, and they blazed in me just as fiercely.

I took a stroll around his room, because I'd never gotten to be in it before. It was decorated very similarly to his library and his lab, all of his usual masculine touches, with only two differences—there was a desk out, holding a lectern with an open book upon it, and there were bags of what looked like gold and gemstones just sitting on the floor.

I went to the book first and thrilled to find his neat handwriting inside—he'd read my journal, so me reading his would only be fair.

I abhor her.
Her beauty, her kindness, her fragility.
The way she engenders me to care for her.
The way I have no choice.

My heart, which'd begun beating so close to the surface moments ago, quickly sank, as I took a step back from the pages. There wasn't a date on them—and I had no way of knowing what day it was besides. But I had to believe the sentiments weren't representative of the current man I knew. I put a hand out, to flip back and read more, then decided not to—what if I only found out more things I didn't want to know? And it was clear he had hated me for a time when I'd first gotten here. It wasn't like he'd tried to hide it.

Just as I had hated him, too...

Only I hadn't written it down anywhere.

I turned and nearly tripped into one of the bags of treasure he had lying about. I caught myself, dipping my hand with the light in it, and caught a familiar twinkling amongst the other glitters. I reached for it and picked it up.

It was my father's favorite ring. The pattern around the outside was unmistakable.

And it was dented, as though it'd maybe been pried off.

When had it come into Rhaim's possession? When he'd delivered my letter? He'd sworn he'd left my father alive, but if he had, why would it be twisted?

I needed to know...but turning back to the bed and seeing Rhaim finally at rest, after being wary for so long, it could wait until tomorrow.

I believed in what we'd been through, and what we had. I was certain there was an adequate explanation and I knew the truth of how I felt for him.

It was a kind of love.

Not the one they wrote about in the books that I'd read, and not the kind that'd ever happened to *Sweet Lirane*, where there were pledges and arches of unicorn horn and pretty dresses and an exciting party: a love born of expediency and noble lineages.

No...whatever we had was stronger than that, and a hundred times more raw.

Rhaim had beaten me to temper me like a legendary sword, and now that I had been, I would be at his side, his to wield, forever.

He wanted to use me, and I craved his hand.

So I crawled into bed naked beside Rhaim in power, knowing that he was mine and I was his. He curved his body around mine readily, wrapping one arm beneath my head, the other around my waist, holding me to his chest like I was meant to be there. He nuzzled his face into my hair, catching it against his beard, and I felt his contented breathing on my neck.

I knew I was where I was meant to be, for the first time in my life, and I, too, fell asleep.

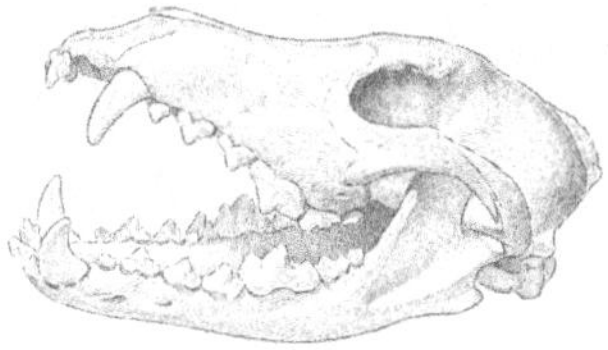

31

RHAIM

I woke, feeling rested for the first time in forever. My arms were empty, but I found a free lock of my hair had been braided when I tried to sweep it out of my face. "Moth—" I complained, at both the braid, and the affront of her having left my bed already.

My bed, that would become *our* bed, soon enough.

It was probably a good thing that she wasn't in bed beside me; otherwise, I'd have never managed to control myself. I had one last thing I wanted to show her before I took her virginity. I took a bath, threaded my piercing back through, then pulled my clothes on to go and find her.

Lisane was in the library, wearing her boy's clothes, curled up in a chair with a book in one hand, a writing stick in her teeth, and the other hand lightly resting on Finx, who was sleeping in her lap. He'd tightly sealed the remaining gap in the wall, and minus some of the other chaos, everything seemed as it had been before the battleship attack had happened, until she looked up and spotted me.

The smile she gave me then shone like the sun and stole my very soul.

And all I wanted to do was imagine a life just like this, streaming out endlessly. Her elegantly slouched in one of my leather chairs, us talking about what we'd read, or things we'd seen, me taking her all over the world, and perhaps us sharing a pipe in front of a fire.

"What?" she asked, watching me, taking the writing stick out.

"Nothing," I said, even though it was a lie.

She was now my *everything*.

And she knew it too, from the rising color on her cheeks. "I'm making a list of places I want to go, and things I want to see," she said, holding up the book in her hand. I recognized the emerald of her journal's cover.

"I see," I said, coming up beside her. "Can I recommend one stop first?"

My moth tilted her head coquettishly. "I suppose," she said, belaboring the word like she was hugely put upon, even as she grinned. "Let me guess. Is it the bedroom?"

I grinned back at her. "No."

"Is it the stable?"

"No."

"Is it the..." She paused, considering.

"Place you won't guess until I show you? Yes, that one."

She laughed and I loved to hear it. "Where is it? Tell me."

"You'll see soon enough."

Her lips puckered. "Am I dressed for the occasion?"

"Perfectly." I waved my hand at the wall, opening the shutters that were still functional, so she could see out, as the castle slowly lowered through dense morning clouds. She tapped Finx, who grumbled but got the hint and then crawled off, so she could rise and run to look out the windows.

"Why are we lowering in another field?"

"Is surprising you always this difficult?" I asked, coming up behind her, wrapping her in my arms. How wonderful it was to feel her sway back into me then, like she knew it was where she belonged.

"Rhaim—what happened to the townspeople?"

I nodded, having known this time would come. “There were some casualties. I didn’t see your little friend amongst the corpses though before we left. I did look for her, for your sake.”

“And...I stopped the Deathless?”

“You did indeed. You flattened the earth they were coming out of. Do you remember that?”

She shook her head against me. “Mostly I just remember wanting them to stop.”

“Well—we will learn more about your magics soon.” The castle reached the ground and settled with a shake.

My moth tilted her head up at me and started to twist in my arms. “Rhaim, how did I—” she started to ask, as Finx ran up the glass excitedly.

“Are those unicorns?” he exclaimed, tilting his head this way and that to look through the windowpane—and his comment instantly claimed Lisane’s attention. She spotted what he did, and gasped.

“Rhaim—” she whispered. I bent my mouth to her ear.

“I brought us to them. It’s a unicorn glade.” The field we’d landed in was filling with the white-horned beasts. I had timed things perfectly—I knew where their herds roamed, and I’d started summoning them ever since we’d been nearing. She looked back at me in disbelief, her question forgotten and her jaw dropped, as I let go of her. "Go get your boots on, moth. We're going outside."

With one more delighted glance out the window, she ran for her bedroom.

"Can I come too?" Finx asked, plastered to the glass.

"Do you have eight little boots?"

"You're not funny," he complained.

I laughed. "You were so patient with the workers, Finx, of course you can come. Just stay by us, and out from underfoot. Try not to scurry, though, horses don't like that."

"Rhaim! Hurry up!" I heard Lisane distantly shouting from below, and I looked to Finx.

"Let's go."

I unlocked the doors to my castle, revealing grazing unicorns in all directions, entirely unbothered by our presence. Lisane took three steps out, then stopped, looking back.

“I shouldn’t be a virgin anymore, Rhaim, not after last night.”

“And yet you still are, somehow, by the slimmest of technicalities.” I strode past her into their herd, and the creatures made irritated noises at me, annoyed by my presence, whereas Lisane got to walk among them. She put a tentative hand out to stroke one’s wide white neck and gasped when it let her.

“They’re beautiful,” she whispered.

“Yes.”

I watched her walk into their midst, petting flanks and necks, stroking her fingers through their silken manes, listening to them whicker about her with contentment. And, oddly, the unicorns were also unconcerned by Finx, who wove amongst them readily. Perhaps they sensed his innocence, too. She turned to beam at me, and I walked forward, making a small wave in the herd as they avoided me, but I stopped before the one she was petting felt the need to move away.

“Enjoy it now, little moth, because after tonight, they will never come to you again. You will be mine, and I will be yours, completely.”

She turned toward me and put a hand to her chest, as if holding her heart in. “Do you mean that?”

"I will never give you reason to doubt." Then she ran for me, flinging her arms around my neck, her amber eyes full of tears. "Why are you crying, little moth?" I asked, catching and steadying her. "Pet the unicorns, not me. I am not going anywhere," I told her, but then she leaned up, her whole body full of expectations, so I bowed my head to kiss her.

And parting her lips with my tongue, pressing in as I held her to me, feeling the give of her body and hearing her make a tiny moan—it felt *right*, in a way that I could not have explained before to anyone.

I would never get to lead Lisane below a unicorn horn arch—nor would I want to, that tradition was abhorrent to me, for many reasons—but kissing her in front of them here felt like making her a life-pledge just the same.

And when I pulled up to tell her as much, I could tell I didn't need to; the shining light of her eyes and her expression said she already knew.

Then, she laughed. "Do we really have to wait until tonight?"

I laughed too, as she drifted in my embrace. "I never thought there'd be a day when I'd be more interesting to a girl than a unicorn."

She spun in my arms to watch the elegant creatures grazing. "Maybe I'll let go of you long enough to ride one."

"You should," I said, urging her forward, just as we both heard Finx shouting.

"Look at me!" he said from a unicorn's back. All eight of his legs were on one of the wider-backed beasts, and he was doing a pleased little dance, tilting his body between them.

"Finx! Get down from there!" I told him, but it was impossible not to grin. The spider-cat laughed and ignored me, bouncing to another unicorn's back. This new one whisked his tail at him, but nothing more. Lisane's laughter pealed, and she ran up to him, asking the unicorn for permission first, before trying to climb aboard.

I wasn't sure the unicorn understood her, but it did tolerate her presence, as she wound her fingers in its mane and threw herself atop it, ungracefully. She wrestled herself upright, and once she was there though, she beamed back at me.

"This is the best surprise I've ever gotten, Rhaim," she said, giving the unicorn's neck a solid thump. "But why do they care so much about virginity?"

"Because magic is often capricious and cruel, like," I said and paused. Now was the time to tell her everything. "Like I used to be. Lisane—" I began and inhaled, finally ready to tell her the story of how she came to be in my castle, but there was a distracting disturbance in the clouds just beyond.

A distinct "R" was appearing in them.

R...for Rhaim?

And then a U appeared beside it.

Sibyi—spelling ***run***.

"Get down, now, and to me," I shouted. I stormed forward, lunging to swipe her off of the unicorn's back, the beasts scattering with surprise.

"Rhaim, what's wrong?" she asked, but I could feel portals opening in a circle—it was too late. I pulled her behind me as mage after mage emerged from them, with a legion of soldiers, and Jaegar astride a normal horse.

"Run with her and die, All-Beast—we will chase you no matter where you go!" he shouted.

I felt Lisane tense and try to look around me. "Father?"

"I have no quarrel with you, Jaegar," I growled at him, my beast already riding beneath my skin. "But it is rich for you to come here, riding a horse, to threaten me." I raised my hand, ready to tell his mount to buck him off and stave his head in, when the girl from town slid off of his horse, from behind him.

"Lirane!" she called out, running forward. "I saw him bite you!" Several unicorns dove out of her path, until she pulled up short, frightened of me.

Jaegar hopped off of his horse as well and stalked forward. "It was one thing, beast, to tolerate our arrangement when you kept to the rules of it, but entirely another to hear rumors of you doing violence to my daughter."

"She is not yours!" I snarled. "She is mine!"

"What is he talking about, Rhaim?" Lisane asked.

"It is no matter," I said, though I knew it was a lie.

"Come away from him, Lisane," her father said, and he beckoned her like a dog. Behind him, soldiers readied their weapons, and those of my kind began to prepare, I could feel magic being readied like electricity. I pulled the remaining unicorns into a tight ring around us, tails in our directions, heads bowed, horns out.

I could hear Lisane's breath quickening. "He...knew where I was...all along? Tell me the truth, Rhaim—"

"Fine. He gave you to me, yes," I spat.

She stepped away from me and it felt like the world was shifting, like when Deathless emerged, only there was nothing breaking except for my heart.

"Why didn't you tell me?" she asked.

I dared to glance at her. "So you wouldn't look at me like that."

Her face was slack with horror, her eyes wide, and her jaw dropped. "Rhaim," she whispered, then turned in a circle, spotting all of her father's men, growing even paler. "Don't hurt him!" she shouted. "I'll come out!"

"Moth," I growled, reaching for her hand, but she yanked it back.

"How dare you?!" she loudly chastised me, and it felt like a slap across my face. "Everything was a lie, and I was your joke," she said, backing up, making the unicorns part, as Finx raced after her. "And to think I almost let you ruin me."

"Do not say those things, Lisane," I hoarsely said, feeling my beast come upon me.

"Or what? Or you'll torture me more?" she challenged.

"Stay by my side and we can fight or flee, but do not abandon me like this." My hold on the unicorns was weakening as my beast rose up. *He* knew how to give chase and *he* wanted to keep her.

She shook her head, moving to her dark-haired friend, and the other girl caught her with open arms. "I could never love you. I could never want to be with you." She pulled something glittering from her pocket and threw it at my feet. I recognized it at once—her father's golden ring. I picked it up, crushing it in my paw. She and her friend reached

Jaegar's side together, and he swept a protective arm around them, her brother standing close behind.

"I never want to see you again, beast!" she shouted back to me. "Live with the knowledge of my hatred in your heart!"

The remaining unicorns scattered as I lost control of them.

Death would've been preferable to this.

"Lisane!" I shouted after her, half a howl, as Castillion stepped forward and portaled her and her entire family away from me. "Don't—!" I called, but it was too late.

She was gone.

And one by one, groups of soldiers and mages also retreated, until I was left baying my heartbreak in the unicorn glade, alone.

Keep reading for a sneak peek of Make Her,
the final book of the Transformation Trilogy.

MAKE HER

TRANSFORMATION TRILOGY BOOK 3

LISANE

For one perfect moment, I was in a unicorn glade, astride one of the proud beasts' backs, smiling down at Rhaim and ready to pledge the rest of my life to him.

I didn't know how to quantify the way that I felt, but I also knew I didn't need to because I knew he felt it too. Something had changed between us last night, vastly for the better. I could tell in all of the actions he'd taken with me this morning, how he felt free to touch me now, but was gentle when he did so. How he teased me, while still giving me a smile.

Finx could create webbing from himself to use to bind things together, and while what Rhaim and I had was not so literal, we had somehow done the same. There was a thread racing from my heart to Rhaim's, growing tighter by the moment, and I knew that it was love.

Then my father came to kill him.

I felt the portals opening around us, only I didn't know what it meant, as Rhaim swept me off of the unicorn and tried to hide me behind himself, and as they were talking, I realized the truth, though I made Rhaim repeat it in my horror: my father had known where I was all along.

And now?

Everything was through.

We were completely outnumbered, and there was only one way for me to save Rhaim's life from my father and his guards.

"Don't hurt him!" I shouted, stepping away from his protection. "I'll come out!"

"Moth," he growled and reached for me, but I yanked away before he could catch hold.

I had to deny everything between us.

Vehemently enough that everyone would believe it.

Even him.

"How dare you?!" I shouted at him, backing up, as tears started streaming down my face, feeling the thread between our hearts grow taut. "Everything was a lie, and I was your joke! And to think I almost let you ruin me!"

I watched my words hit Rhaim like so many blows. "Do not say those things, Lisane," he pleaded.

"Or what?" I asked him, begging him to understand, to know that I would choose a life without windows for a thousand years, as long as I knew he was safe. "Or you'll torture me more?"

"Stay by my side and we can fight or flee, but do not abandon me like this," he growled, obliviously.

I ran for Jelena and she caught me with open arms. "I could never love you!" I shouted back at him, knowing I was lying. "I could never want to be with you!"

And then I plucked my father's ring I'd found among his treasures from a pocket and threw it at him. It was the only clue I could give him that I was doing this intentionally—that I had figured out some small piece of my own captivity the prior night and that it hadn't mattered to me.

Because every moment of this morning among the unicorns, here, with him, had been true, and I would treasure the memory of it for the rest of my candle-lit days.

Jelena grabbed me, and then my father did, and I could feel the thin thread in my heart begin to fray. "I never want to see you again, beast!" I screamed, sobbing, and I saw Rhaim surging forward on instinct, changing into his monstrous form to take me back, even if it cost him his life. "Live with the knowledge of my hatred in your heart!" I shrieked to repel him—and it worked.

He stopped—mid-step, mid-change—and the thread between us snapped.

Rhaim didn't dare take my love for granted, even though he ought.

Even though I knew I would love him helplessly, until the end of the world.

I stepped into the cold dark of Castillion's portal, knowing I would never have my freedom again, but at least Rhaim was alive, hearing him, still half a beast, broken-heartedly howling my name.

RHAIM

Lisane was gone.

Of her own volition.

And I was alone like I would always be until she someday took pity on me and came back and killed me.

Or maybe I died, dreaming of her face.

Because I didn't know what was left for me now.

I fell to my knees in the middle of the glade, all of the unicorns scattering as I panted, unable to manage the intensity of my pain.

Lisane was gone, and at no time had I even begun to plan for this possibility, the one where I gave my heart to a girl and she tore it to pieces before disappearing. I had been hurt by innumerable creatures while learning their ways, been pierced and poisoned, bitten and burnt, but nothing I'd ever encountered had ever destroyed me so utterly as this: my little moth, fluttering away.

Denying me—and everything we had.

Had I been a fool? And Lisane the world's most impressive actress?

Or had the sudden realization that I'd played even a minor role in her kidnapping truly turned her against me?

I didn't know, and I couldn't hold back my base nature any longer. I couldn't stand to be a man if it meant hurting like this.

Let *him* be in charge of me.

Let *him* be the one in agony.

Because I—I did not want to feel anymore.

Or ever again.

I went wild and shifted, letting my beast take me over.

YOU'LL NEVER GUESS HOW LISANE AND RHAIM'S STORY ENDS. FIND OUT IN MAKE HER, THE FINAL BOOK IN THE TRANSFORMATION TRILOGY, RELEASING AUGUST 15, 2023

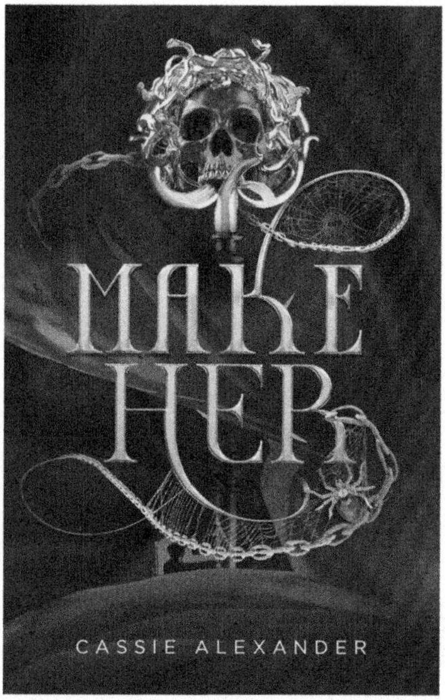

In the meantime, be sure to join Cassie's mailing list for secret scenes, character art, and extra stories!

ALSO BY CASSIE ALEXANDER

Check out cassiealexander.com for content & trigger warnings.

The Dark Ink Tattoo Series

Blood of the Pack

Blood at Dusk

Blood at Midnight

Blood at Moonlight

Blood at Dawn

Blood of the Dead

The Longest Night (Bonus Story)

Edie Spence Series

Nightshifted

Moonshifted

Shapeshifted

Deadshifted

Bloodshifted

Transformation Trilogy

Bend Her

Break Her

Make Her

The Prince of the Other Worlds Series (Written with Kara Lockharte)

Dragon Called

Dragon Destined

Dragon Fated

Dragon Mated

Dragons Don't Date (Short Story)

Bewitched (Bonus Story)

The Wardens of the Other Worlds Series

Dragon's Captive

Wolf's Princess

Wolf's Rogue

Dragon's Flame

Standalone Stories

AITA?

Her Ex-boyfriend's Werewolf Lover

Her Future Vampire Lover

The House

Rough Ghost Lover

ABOUT THE AUTHOR

Cassie Alexander is a registered nurse and author. She's written numerous paranormal romances, sometimes with her friend Kara Lockharte. She lives in the Bay Area with one husband, two cats, and one million succulents.

Sign up for Cassie's mailing list at cassiealexander.com/newsletter to get free books, bonus scenes, even more character art, and cat photos!

facebook.com/CassieAlexanderReaders
twitter.com/cassie_author
instagram.com/authorcassiealexander

Made in the USA
Columbia, SC
13 May 2023

16585457R00170